EQUILATERAL

EQUILATERAL

A NOVEL

Ken Kalfus

BLOOMSBURY

New York   London   New Delhi   Sydney

The author wishes to thank the Pew Fellowships in the Arts and the John Simon Guggenheim Memorial Foundation. He also wishes to acknowledge his extravagant use of Google Books, Wikipedia, Wolfram Alpha, and Starry Night, a product of the Simulation Curriculum Corp.

The author is grateful to James Stockard and Sally Young, of the Loeb Fellowship at the Harvard Graduate School of Design, for many courtesies during his wife's 2011–12 fellowship year.

Copyright © 2013 by Ken Kalfus

Published by Bloomsbury USA, New York

All papers used by Bloomsbury USA are natural, recyclable products made from wood grown in well-managed forests. The manufacturing processes conform to the environmental regulations of the country of origin.

LIBRARY OF CONGRESS CATALOGING-IN-PUBLICATION DATA HAS BEEN APPLIED FOR.

ISBN: 978-1-62040-006-7

FIRST U.S. EDITION 2013

1 3 5 7 9 10 8 6 4 2

Typeset by Westchester Book Group
Printed in the United States by Thomson-Shore, Inc. Dexter, Michigan

FOR INGA AND SKY

Astonishing! Everything is intelligent!

PYTHAGORAS OF SAMOS

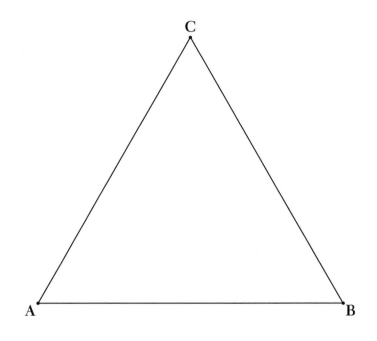

ONE

B ound by the Qattara Depression in the north and the Gilf Kebir Plateau in the south, Dakhla Oasis in the east and fabled Cyrenaica in the west, the central portion of the vastness known as Bahr ar Rimal al 'Azim, or the Great Sand Sea, may be reached in eight days by caravan on the Concession track from the steam packet port of Nag Hammadi. At Point A, a shimmering, heat-warped village or town that exists in the absence of a water source or any natural conditions that would make it attractive or even sufficient for human habitation, our journey ends. There we find a sprawling encampment comprised of tents, brick and mud shelters, earth-moving machinery, wet-eyed beasts of burden, and a swarm of dusky men mostly stripped to their waists. In the fever of the day the men scream recondite obscenities at the camels and the mules and especially, most viciously and most creatively, at each other.

As rude and tumultuous as it may seem to those who have just arrived, the city is only the fulcrum of a tremendous manual exertion. Around the encampment, spread over barrens that occupy thousands of square miles, hundreds of thousands of other men are scattered into work gangs. They have spades. They dig furiously into the sand and loose dirt, banking the debris on either side of their excavations. The excavations appear to be exceedingly wide roadways into which a lining of pitch is being laid, yet it's not obvious what conveyances they will bear or to where. The men certainly don't know, despite repeated instruction.

This is Professor Sanford Thayer's empire, cast under a pitiless star. He can barely drag himself from his camp bed to defy his physicians. At the opening of the tent he gazes upon the settlement and dwells, for the space of a tremor, on the drive and the daring, the decades of work and the moments of impulse, the mountains of paperwork and the massifs of cash, that have brought these animals, this machinery, and these men into the field of his famously acute vision. In that tremor two sentiments take up arms and rise against each other.

The first combatant is despair: despair at his own folly, despair at the workers' incompetence, despair at the human primitiveness that mocks the greatest accomplishments of industry and culture.

But despair is dealt a wounding blow. Consider the nobility of this striving, by mule and man. Consider man's ingenuity. Consider this project as a pure, uncompromised expression of human intelligence. Progress is slow, but the endeavor approaches completion. It *will* be completed. The fourth planet, high above the horizon in Sagittarius, unseen behind the screen of day, will be visible in the hours before morning dusk tomorrow, a fierce, unquenchable ember.

TWO

He knows few words of Arabic, that brittle, uvula-stretching language, but he knows the word for the number fifty, *khamsin*, which is also the name for the fifty-day season of stale, heavy winds that are discharged from the Sudanese wastes in the months of March, April, and May. Their sands scour and penetrate, carve mountains, raise dunes, disfigure faces and snouts, and beat down every possible insanely quixotic tendril of vegetation. Clothes and canvas are torn and dissolved. The sky assumes a venomous shade of yellow. Grains of sand prick Thayer's eyes, even when his eyes are shut, each grain an irritation and a rebuke. The fellahin tell stories of men lost in the *khamsin*, flayed to their skeletons, yet still leading the remnants of their dromedaries, searching for shelter, still trying to read their demagnetized compasses.

The wind from the south raises the temperature twenty degrees, but he dares not open the flaps to his tent. At night the *khamsin* chuffs and scrapes at the canvas; he may be startled by faraway rumblings like the sound of furniture being moved. The winds are relentless, except when they stop. Then he realizes he's being suffocated in the heat.

Thayer's eyepieces are wrapped in lambskin leather, placed within fitted tins, and then packed in Chinese cedar cabinets built to his specifications. Yet a single grain of sand, every edge daggered, makes it past these defenses. Lifting it from the surface of the lens requires the most exquisite care, and the employ of a tiny baby's breath nebulizer. Only Thayer is permitted to attempt it. Even then the damage may have already been done, by the original descent of the grain to the surface of the glass or afterward by minute seismic forces that have rocked the particle into the glass's unseen spaces and crevices. A light-splitting track is gouged.

△

The call to prayer comes five times a day and the Mohammedans drop where they are. We're surprised every time. The muezzin's cry is always preceded by a moment of intense quiet; once the call comes, the foreign visitor can't recall what he was thinking in that moment, no matter how desperately he seeks it. He can't speak over the muezzin, nor around him, nor decipher his lyric. The call of the muezzin is something deeper and older than the lyric, from before language. The cry promises knowledge without reason and truths that are hidden within rote phrasings and tautologies ("There is no God but God"; "Blessed are the blessed") obscure to the Western mind.

Thayer hears it and writhes in his camp bed.

△

Wilson Ballard, the chief engineer, tells Thayer that when he came in a few moments ago the astronomer was talking in his sleep, but that he couldn't make out what he was trying to say.

Thayer recalls some fierce dreaming: thoughts and convictions that riveted his soul. He doesn't remember their actual content, only their intensity.

Now that Thayer's awake, Ballard is back to business. He occupies a chair at the foot of the camp bed, sipping a drink. It appears to be an iced drink. Radiant geometric solids slowly turn within the liquid, their facets throwing off sparks. But the nearest ice is in the bar at Shepheard's Hotel in Cairo, precisely 488 miles and 972 yards 51.21 degrees east of north. So it can't be ice.

"There's been talk of a strike," Ballard says. "I suppose we have agitators underfoot—or very likely Daoud Pasha is looking for more baksheesh. I don't think anything will come of it, but we're already behind, especially on Side AC."

The girl hid herself the moment Ballard entered the tent, yet Thayer knows she's near. She has some native odor, a perfume, some inner resonance, an aura that remains detectable. He tries to look past the engineer, but once he moves his head the planet finds a fresh axis on which to spin. He closes his eyes. Still the Earth revolves, so that his feet gyre above his head.

"What do they want?"

"More money," Ballard replies. "Better food. To be white men. I don't know."

"But when they protest, what do they say? How do they express their grievances?"

Ballard is accustomed to these kinds of questions from Thayer, the man who looks for meaning everywhere, even in the stars.

Thayer is not suited to the East, to its enigmas, to the desert and its great expanse of nonmeaning, to peoples for whom literal meaning is irrelevant and perhaps even an insult to God. Thayer is always asking why. In the East the world and its manifold mechanics are simply *what*. Ballard shrugs.

"They're digging now."

"Do you have what you need?"

Ballard doesn't reply.

"Are there enough spades? Enough water? Why are we so far behind?"

Gently, since the candor itself is sufficiently brutal, the engineer says, "June the seventeenth won't be met, Sanford. You'll have to cable London."

Anger shrouds Thayer's vision and engraves a line of pain from behind his eyebrows to the interior of his right temple, much worse than what has seemed unbearable for the past three days. *These fools!* He staggers under the weight of the stupidity (mentally, mentally, keeping the outward calm that has sustained him for a decade). The Earth will be at maximum eastern elongation on June 17, her greatest angular distance from the sun, a fact central to every proposal, scheme, and design that he has ever put forward. Yet Ballard still doesn't appreciate the urgency of the date. Even at the Concession, even in Sir Harry's offices, the urgency remains theoretical, mathematical. It's something an astronomer is telling them. They know he has charts that support the supreme importance of June 17, as well as geometric calculations and proofs, but the evidence remains intangible, only a celestial notion.

"The appointment is immovable," he declares, exhausting the last of his strength.

Ballard swirls the liquid in his glass and Thayer records a distinct clink.

"They're breaking the equipment," Ballard says. "They break the sand carts, they break the water tankers, they break the spades. It takes genius and diligent effort to break a spade."

"If we miss maximum elongation . . ." Thayer mutters.

"We'll be well situated for weeks after." The engineer claims to know something about astronomy. He once navigated the Empty Quarter with a hoop sextant and a secondhand ephemeris bought in the Aden bazaar.

"The Flare is half the endeavor."

"Only half. And if we're a little late—"

"It won't make sense to them!"

"It will, Sanford . . ."

Thayer's eyelids flicker shut. Even in the darkened tent, the light's killing him. Light has always been his comfort, streaming down from the heavens. Now every glint, glimmer, and stray beam, no matter how suffused, rests on his sight like a splinter. Where's the girl? She's close. She's aware of his pain.

"We're making every possible effort," Ballard insists, suddenly severe with the astronomer, the man he admires above all others. Sanford Thayer is the Equilateral's inspiration and its motive force, its high priest, and its secular, public face, a face recognizable to millions around the world. He's just as indispensable to the Equilateral's completion as he believes. But the chief engineer does not answer to Thayer, despite the astronomer's influence with Sir Harry, nor to Thayer's private secretary, who oversees every facet of the project. With consent of the governors, Harry may dismiss Ballard at any time and exact financial penalties for the project's shortcomings, including its failure to be completed by June 17. There are contractual considerations that Ballard must always keep in mind, as he has learned in the course of a storied career in which the principals were often distant from the structures being raised. As an engineer, he knows that forces and stresses are not always material.

Yet no human rationalization, no history of obstacles faced or surmounted, no catalogue of human weakness, no glum survey of Eastern conditions, and no telegraphic eloquence will overturn the constants of planetary motion. Thayer won't send the cable.

△

Ballard has left. Despite the midday heat and his fragility, despite the girl's murmured entreaties, Thayer again struggles from his camp bed, shuffles toward the tent's opening, and pulls back the flap. He wants to see what the engineer was talking about— the petulant workers, the spoiled machinery—but everything material has been washed from the visible spectrum in the fulsome light. His pupils can't sufficiently contract. And the desert is as empty and cold as interplanetary space.

THREE

Two years earlier they had arrived at this place, a point determined by sextant and chronometer, at 25 degrees 40' 26" north latitude, 25 degrees 10' 6" east longitude. "Point A!" Thayer declared. Two hundred sixty men and one woman dismounted.

No man-made structure was visible from one horizon to the next. They knew there were none for many horizons beyond. Nor was there evidence of vegetation. The only significant geographical feature gently upwelled in the south, a rise of perhaps thirty feet. Here, where the easternmost part of the Libyan Desert slides into the western expanses of the Egyptian Khedivate, the Great Sand Sea was like a page of untouched foolscap. Thayer surveyed the desolation with supreme satisfaction, even a shudder of triumph. Although a single spade had yet to cleave the sands, he congratulated himself, after an arduous decade-long campaign, for having summoned into his employ the vast resources—financial, political, and scientific—that had transported them to this until-now remote location.

He called for the dowsers, hoping against hope.

No water was found, but within weeks Point A had been

established as a settlement, its walls of canvas rippling against the winds. Caravans arrived daily, from Nag Hammadi and Alexandria. Descending from their mounts, the drivers' desert-scorched faces betrayed awe, disapproval, and an impatience to be paid and be gone. Hundreds of men were soon quartered and dispatched to erect quarters for thousands more. The men swore while machinery groaned, cables sang themselves taut, and camels brayed. Thayer surveyed the activity, as even-tempered as always, consulting with Ballard as the preparations unspooled onto the desert floor from blueprints drawn in London.

In those several weeks so much effort was expended, so many challenges were overcome, and such bitter sacrifices were made that it was painful for some to contemplate that these were only the preliminary tasks being accomplished, and that each would generate myriad labors further. The commencement ceremonies were assigned to the twenty-ninth day of April 1892—the second of the Mohammedan month of Shawwal 1309. High officials from six European countries, the United States, Egypt, and the Sublime Porte were summoned to this exercise, along with lords of industry and finance and senior ecclesiastics. Although these men sent representatives of modest rank, mostly second vice consuls and assistant concessionaires, neither the envoys' low status and heat fatigue nor the bleakness of the environment could diminish the proceedings' pageantry and historic gravity. An Egyptian royal band in full military dress played the anthem of each participating nation, as well as selections from Bizet and Offenbach, the horns glaring under the morning, then noonday, then afternoon sun.

Before making his remarks, Thayer stepped out from under the canopy that provided shade to the Europeans. The sudden passage into the sun made him look, for a moment, like a man on fire. He *was* a man on fire, and not because of the sun.

"Gentlemen," Thayer began, looking out over the toweled heads of the fellahin. They shifted warily in their sandals and loin wraps, uncertain why the dragomen had interrupted their work to assemble them there. They had demanded and received assurances that they would be paid for the day. "My friends," Thayer added, with further generosity.

He thanked every official who had contributed to the endeavor, whether present or not. He recalled the strenuous, much-opposed campaign, from the moment of its conception in his Cambridge study, to the cautious and fraught acceptance by his colleagues, to the gratifying, unprecedented outpouring of public support, to the Khedive's far-seeing, gracious awarding of the Concession, to the surveyors' courageous expeditions across unexplored desert, to the first structures raised at Point A. He paid respect to the Ottoman Sultan, these sands' nominal sovereign. He praised the governors in London.

He concluded:

"What we will accomplish here in the coming months and years will prove the supreme and definitive achievement of our times. The century has already witnessed the mixing of ocean waters, the erection of ziggurats that dwarf biblical towers, cities of churning millions, instantaneous telegraphy between the continents, the spreading of civilization to the world's darkest regions, and, in an increasing number of countries, introduction of the universal franchise. With all due respect to the admirable men who executed these endeavors, they cannot measure up to ours, neither in scale, nor in invested capital, nor in physical effort, nor, especially, in the benefits to be reaped by mankind. For this undertaking has no equal. Our intellects, our hearts, our muscles, and our common faith in the Creator will ensure that the century will close here, on this sterile plain, with the first communication from the leading men of our planet, across the chasm of space, to the most intelligent inhabitants of another."

The astronomer wasn't exaggerating the scope of the enterprise and never has, not in his first letter on the subject to *Philosophical Transactions*, nor in the papers subsequent, nor in the countless Sunday supplement interviews to which he has submitted. As of today, nine hundred thousand men labor to realize his vision, shifting the frozen currents of the Great Sand Sea, two hundred thousand more than the numbers employed in the excavation of the Suez Canal thirty years earlier. Thousands are in fact either veterans of Suez or the sons and grandsons of veterans; they are descendants, too, of pyramid-builders. According to Thayer's calculations, to which he has brought the same rigor as to those with which he has determined occultations, quadratures, elongations, and disk illumination, they will have excavated 1,027 billion cubic feet of sand upon the enterprise's successful completion. The men are committed to putting down 4,605 square miles of shallow pitch, produced in the constantly running factories located at Point A, Point B, and Point C. The Concession's petroleum use, twenty-two million English barrels pumped from newly discovered fields in Arabia, Mesopotamia, and Persia and transported to the Equilateral by pipeline laid for this purpose, surpasses the total amount that has ever been extracted from the Near East. It will be consumed in a single night. A dozen men have already given their lives for this project, several in harrowing circumstances.

The financial effort has been no less heroic. As of this date the Mars Concession has been capitalized at sixteen million pounds sterling, twice as much as Suez, funded by massive state expenditure and private investment, not least the collection of small coins from the schoolchildren of six nations, their ha'pennies, sous, and pfennigs inserted into the slots of thousands of little tin boxes emblazoned with Giovanni Schiaparelli's most revealing map. It has drawn extravagantly from the coffers of several European and American banks. It may draw from them again. Demanding cooperation among rival governments and financial enterprises from one end of the civilized world to the other, the Equilateral is the greatest international peacetime undertaking in the history of man. It has spawned new legislation, new protocols, and new treaties. In the marshaling of human resources regardless of national origin, it suggests the only possible future for human life on Earth, even though its every single effort is, in the final analysis, destined to be apprehended far from terrestrial soil.

The geometry to which Professor Sanford Thayer has devoted his genius will initially consist of a single simple figure, a triangle whose sides are equal. This figure, so easy to draw on a sheet of foolscap, requires more vigorous exertion when carved into the desert, each side 306 miles and 1,663 yards in length, precisely 1/73rd of the Earth's circumference at Base AB's latitude, each side a trench five miles in width. Further labor is required to pave the trenches with pitch, and then to pour a twelve-inch layer of petroleum on their surfaces. In a series of computations confirmed by the world's leading astronomers, Thayer has determined that in daytime the desert's perfect black triangle cast upon the white sands, incontrovertible proof of terrestrial intelligence, will be visible to indigenous observers equipped with telescopes on the planet Mars. Their attention will be seized. Then sometime before dawn on June 17, 1894, at the moment of Earth's most favorable position in the Martian sky, the petroleum pooled in the trenches on each side of the Equilateral will be ignited simultaneously, launching a Flare from the Earth's darkened limb that across millions of miles of empty space will petition for man's membership in the fraternity of planetary civilizations.

FOUR

The Italian astronomer Giovanni Schiaparelli, observing the planet Mars from the Brera Observatory in Milan during its 1877 approach, was the first to discern water-bearing channels, or what he termed *canali*, on its surface. In the English-language press, the word was invariably translated as "canals," suggesting that their provenance was artificial. Schiaparelli and his colleagues at first cautioned the public against a hasty interpretation, but, peering through the atmospheric haze of the two planets in subsequent close encounters, they saw that each waterway was cut geometrically along a great circle: the shortest, most efficient distance from one point on a sphere to another, just as one would expect if the channels were purposefully excavated. The seasonal thickening and darkening of the lands adjacent to the channels implied the vernal germination of irrigated crops, like the famous greening of Egyptian fields after they've been inundated by the Nile every year. Circular regions of growth bloomed at the canals' intersections, which were evidently desert oases. The waterways' growth from one opposition to the next revealed ongoing excavations that far surpass Austria's abyssal Adelbert Mine, the railway tunnel beneath the River Severn, the Kiel Canal, the Suez Canal, and the other massive earth-moving projects that have challenged this century's terrestrial engineers.

The popular imagination was inflamed, as we may recall. The papers issued bulletins describing a civilization in its thirst-wracked death throes, struggling for survival. Poets apotheosized the planet: the American Oliver Wendell Holmes described "the snows that glittered on the disk of Mars"; his compatriot Henry Wadsworth Longfellow reflected: "And earnest thought within me rise, / When I behold afar, / Suspended in the evening skies, / The shield of that red star." Romances, operettas, military marches, dramas and masques, ballets, political polemics and satires, music hall lectures, and religious sermons employed Mars as a subject, a metaphor, an exemplar, a prop, and a foil. An advertisement for Pears' soap in the *Illustrated London News* portrayed an elegantly robed copper-hued Martian beauty performing her toilet on the edge of a shimmering watercourse plied by gondolas. In Paris, the great patissier Louis-Ernest Ladurée offered a strawberry-cream-filled profiterole that he called Le Sang du Mars.

While tempering the public's most extravagant speculation and expectation, science soberly confirmed the evidence for Martian life. Indeed, the presumption that intelligence was confined to our trivial little globe was shown to be as simply minded Earth-centered as the pre-Copernican notion that the sun, moon, and planets turned around it. In the following decade, every twenty-six months when the two planets approached each other, celebrated astronomers like Camille Flammarion and Hector France-Lanord built on Schiaparelli's observations of a vast

Martian irrigation network. Leading scientists, philosophers, and politicians, as well as ordinary men, contemplated communication with the fourth planet—but only one man possessed the audacity, persistence, and powers of persuasion to effectuate a plan for making contact.

The press amplified every one of Thayer's proposals; the public clamored to have them answered. Bankers met with statesmen. Foreign secretaries gathered. An agreement was reached with the Khedive of Egypt to establish a "concession," a consortium of private and public interests that would assume responsibility for excavating the Equilateral on Egyptian soil. Sir Harry was named to lead a Board of Governors from every participating nation. Treaties, protocols, codicils, and memoranda were signed, some of them necessarily as removed from public scrutiny as certain celestial objects. To establish a chancellery from which to direct the labors that were to be expended on the Great Sand Sea, the Mars Concession took possession of a three-story gray brick palace in Pall Mall, designed by Sir Christopher Wren during the reign of Queen Anne. Important men of government, finance, and enterprise now roam its shadowed, chandeliered hallways. Great oak doors are firmly shut. Documents are copied and filed. Telegraphic messages are dispatched day and night.

Thayer has visited Mars House but once, to pay a courtesy call on Sir Harry.

FIVE

While the astronomer tumbles back to his sickbed to dream of Ballard's latest report, allowing it to swirl and sink within the currents of his fever, his private secretary, Miss Adele Keaton, is engaged elsewhere in Point A, at the transport bureau, where there are troubling discrepancies in the accounts. "Eight tankers went out, but only one came back," Miss Keaton observes, gazing hard at the Turkish bookkeeper.

The young man blinks beneath his tarbush.

"What do you say to that?"

"Madam?"

"Last Wednesday eight full water tankers were dispatched to the crews at mile one-seventeen on Side AB. Only one returned. What happened to the other seven?"

The Turk doesn't reply, apparently surprised by her powers of speech. Miss Keaton, who's wearing a sun hat and a long white muslin dress, recognizes that the man is uncomfortable talking to an unmarried woman, especially about a professional matter, even though she regularly comes to review the books. She knows that the bookkeeper's hiding behind his discomfort to avoid answering the question. Now he buries a long finger into his glossy mustache and slides the finger slowly beneath his nose. Is this a sign? Is it a rank provocation or a nervous mannerism? Miss Keaton studies the ledger. She will have to dispatch a courier to Point B in the event that the drivers were sent there in error, but she knows the missing tankers, and their drivers, are not at Point B. They won't be at Point C either. Seven thousand five hundred gallons of water have gone missing.

△

When she stops in to see Thayer, he has clearly declined. His head is sunk into his pillow, while his eyes have receded into their sockets. He appears exhausted.

He murmurs, "Ballard says . . ."

Dismayed, she turns sharply to glare at the girl, who has been standing at the foot of the bed, holding a pitcher. Bint lowers her eyes.

"Mr. Ballard says many things," Miss Keaton snaps. "Not all of them to his credit. Dr. McKinnon has prescribed sleep and rest. Let's keep that foremost." She rearranges Thayer's pillows and says, more softly, "A convoy of fresh men arrived at Point B yesterday. They're already in the field."

She turns to the girl and with her hands together leans the side of her head against them. She repeats, "Sleep and rest. Sleep and rest."

The girl nods uncertainly. Miss Keaton wonders if she thinks she's telling her to pray.

She takes another look at Thayer before leaving and then

walks the few paces to her office within the warren of attached tents and mud-brick structures that comprises the Equilateral's chief administrative compound.

△

Miss Keaton is fully trusted as the single individual capable of keeping the entire scope of the undertaking, theoretical and practical, within her field of view. She inspects the daily reports, issuing questions and demands for clarification in Thayer's name, and she corresponds directly with London from Point A's telegraphic station, whose cable extends 510 miles to the bureau of the Eastern Telegraph Company in Alexandria. She's well aware of the excavation's difficulties. She believes they can be resolved through more dedicated, more intelligent application of effort. June the seventeenth can still be met, if Ballard will only properly manage his men.

Even while performing her administrative duties, the secretary continues to take Thayer's dictation and frequently composes arguments in his name, reiterating the evidence for the Martian canals and for the Equilateral's inevitability—and not only for its inevitability but also for its necessity, and not only for its necessity but also for its perfect crystalline beauty. She responds to newspaper inquiries, the more foolish with the most patience. She can knock down his opponents with as much force as if Thayer himself threw the punch.

The range of nonterrestrial phenomena are delimited by her computations no less than the quantities of soil removed and foodstuffs consumed. She can foretell precisely the elliptical, elegant, careening loop-the-loops performed by the planets in their traces. She turns declinations into azimuths; looking up from the page, she counts off the hours of right ascension. She has seen the canals and, viewing from the twenty-four-inch Cassegrain reflector at Thayer's private observatory in Kent, she discovered the 1890 completion of the waterway between Elysium and Trivium Charontis. Thayer calls the verdant, newly irrigated region Keatonia. He has labeled it that on every map issued from his drawing table.

The secretary comprehends what the canals imply, in all their promise and dread. While Thayer originated the idea of the Equilateral on his own over many years of brooding consideration, Miss Keaton had been his first audience, listening to his proposal in rapt silence. She responded with shrewd, succinct refinements.

Miss Keaton's office is dominated by a large pedestal desk and four oak filing cabinets. The Concession's sectional maps of the Western Desert are fastened to the walls of the tent. They've been marked heavily. Although the missing tankers have receded from present concern, Miss Keaton has returned quivering. With no one to observe her, she lays her head on the desk. She's soaked under her arms and in the small of the back. Her stays chafe. She wishes she could fully immerse herself in a bath.

Thayer's illness has been a blow to them all. He looked awful this afternoon. The engineer should never have been allowed into his sickroom. Miss Keaton has of course kept Thayer informed of the delays, while exercising a certain degree of tact. Ballard is incapable of this tact, either with Thayer or with anyone else.

Miss Keaton blames Bint for the intrusion. She knows she's

being unfair, for the slight, quiet girl can't possibly assume the authority to turn away the chief engineer. She can hardly speak a word of English. But the secretary believes that, once entrusted with Thayer's care, Bint should, must, exercise powers beyond those of her birth or station. Either that or Miss Keaton will have to remain with Thayer while he's ill and water tankers will continue to go astray, segments of piping will remain unconnected, accounts will be overdrawn, men will be sent into the desert without spades, and the Equilateral will never be done.

△

A man requires two quarts of drinking water per day. A man performing arduous physical labor in subtropical desert heat requires five quarts, though the Egyptians, acclimated to the arid conditions of their homeland, can survive on three and a half quarts. Nine hundred thousand fellahin performing these labors thus require 787,500 gallons of water every day, which must be delivered to them at their work sites, brought directly to their ever-parched lips. Some of the drinking water has been obtained by draining the few springs that lie beneath the Western Desert, but most has to be transported from the Nile, the land's munificent all-provider, along an aqueduct constructed by the Concession and guarded against diversion by its troops. The conduit terminates at Point B, where the water is funneled into mule-drawn tankers, which are then dispatched to the work sites along the Equilateral's perimeter.

The water vanishes within the nine hundred thousand men. Tomorrow another 787,500 gallons will have to be delivered.

In the desert a laborer requires refreshment every two hours. Without it he weakens. Without it his mind turns from work. He bends into his spade visualizing a chilled pool. He lifts the spade and imagines the ocean he has never seen. He deposits the sand dreaming of rain showers, of purling streams, of the Nile's cataracts, and of a marbled city whose every plaza and square is built around a gushing, splashing fountain. His saliva turns adhesive and his breathing becomes hurried, closely pursued by a weak, rapid pulse. His skin is hot and dry to the touch, almost papery. He becomes dizzy. He will faint. A man in the desert without water will die in very short order.

The lines of the Equilateral pass through landscapes drained of color and life. No desert scrub clots upon the hills. Turn over a rock and no reptile emerges. The morning sun rises unaccompanied by birdsong. The heat pours down in a torrent. From time to time the foremen lock the water tankers until the assigned quantity of sand has been excavated.

The open-minded reader may envisage another land whose waters are scarce, a dying land where the acquisition of a substance that he takes for granted is its inhabitants' greatest imperative. The reader may contemplate creatures thirsty from the moment they are born to the moment they expire. In distant epochs they developed religious doctrines whose fires of fanaticism were stoked by this quest for water, faiths whose priests transported containers of water to places of adoration. The wars that have been fought over this cracked, blistered land—all of them essentially civil wars, each of them a struggle for simple existence—provoked brutalities that dwell on the race's conscience forever. But as the water shortage becomes now even more acute, these destructive impulses have been subsumed. The contest has become a supremely civilized one. It depends on worldwide cooperation, the rational organization of the classes of labor, individual altruism, the promotion of the sciences, and the elevation of irrigation science as the highest art.

Thayer has seen this planet of heroes, pale and fragile, trembling in his eyepiece.

SIX

Only weeks earlier, as Earth and Mars moved into position on the same side of the sun, Thayer woke in a severe ague-fit, beginning with chills in the small of his back. Soon he was shivering down the length of his body and couldn't rise from bed. Point A's chief physician and three of his colleagues were summoned. They found him in a high fever. After examining his eyes and tongue, they left the tent to consult among themselves. A few minutes later Dr. McKinnon stepped in and asked Miss Keaton for permission to speak with her outside.

"Our consensus is that the fever most likely originates in a malarial process."

Miss Keaton peered at him, trying to gauge the extent of his equivocation.

The doctor added, "The effects will pass. We can expect that he'll return to his duties."

"He'll recover?"

Dr. McKinnon smiled, a gesture that brought the worried creases around his eyes into relief. Miss Keaton thought she saw fear. "We're prescribing rest and a course of quinine. If the effects of the illness return, it may not be for months or years."

He added, "Professor Thayer is indispensable. He'll be provided with the best care possible."

They left the astronomer in poor condition. His eyes were dull and he was too weak to leave his camp bed. Dissembling her own anxiety, Miss Keaton crisply issued orders to move her office adjacent to his sickroom. When they were alone, she told him, "Good work, Pho. You're a true son of the desert now."

Since Thayer fell ill, Miss Keaton has developed a low opinion of Point A's physicians. They staff the infirmary and seem capable of treating the occasional cuts and bruises and mangled limbs brought in by the excavators, and they may detect malingerers, yet they have no systematic way of identifying and treating illness. They demonstrate little familiarity with tropical disease or even tropical heat, donning the same waistcoats as they did in London, Berlin, and Vienna. The physicians themselves are often flushed and short of breath.

Every morning and evening they return to confer in hushed voices, deferring to each other according to their seniority, professional attainment, and deportment. The doctors offer uncertain remedies and Miss Keaton gradually realizes that, although the field of medicine may heal and bring comfort, it's unconstrained by the rigors of measurement and logic, unlike any science with which she's familiar. Some observations of Thayer's condition are ignored because they don't conform to expectation; treatments are prescribed without empirical evidence that they correspond to the underlying illness; they're discarded before they've been proven ineffective. She cloaks her anger. Assembling in Thayer's sickroom two weeks after he first fell ill, the physicians agree again that Thayer is suffering from malaria.

There are murmurs of emphatic concurrence, amplified by averments in regards to etiology and symptomatology, followed by further concurrences. Then one of the doctors says, under his breath, to no one in particular, not even, it seems, to himself, that Thayer's ailment may very well prove to be Kharga Fever.

The doctors are correct, however, in their expectation that the symptoms will pass. One morning a week after Ballard's unfortunate visit, Thayer emerges in full desert kit, including military boots, khaki pants, a belted jacket, and a pith helmet. The color has returned to his face. Bint has given him a close shave and trimmed his brief red-brown mustache. The astronomer surveys the immediate neighborhood around his quarters. He's disappointed that tents have gone slack and an unattended spade is buried to its shaft, but in the distance he can make out the blackness of the Vertex cutting into the horizon, and a pool of quicksilver miraging above it. He strides into Miss Keaton's office and announces his intention to ride along Side AC out to mile 270.

Studying figures from the Point B pitch factory, she hasn't heard him come in. She looks up now, surprised. He grins slyly.

Miss Keaton says, "It's been taken care of."

The diggers at mile 270, about forty miles from Point A, have encountered some limestone that escaped the notice of the surveyors, not the first rock or high dune or other impediment to do so. Ballard dispatched a blasting crew yesterday. She mentioned the problem last evening, but didn't think Thayer heard her.

"Have they broken through?"

"There's no reason for you to be there. If you're well enough, you should write to Professor France-Lanord about the shadowing in Mare Australe."

"The letter can wait," Thayer insists. "I'll be up and back by dinner."

"You need to rest."

An offended surprise momentarily occults his features. She realizes that he won't acknowledge that he's been ill, or that he's been in bed with a fever. Or that the entire camp was made gravely anxious. Or that the Concession's shares fell in London. She was obliged to cable daily bulletins directly to Sir Harry.

She says cautiously, "You feel well?"

"Of course I do."

He stands before her in his natural easygoing defiance, his chest out, his chin tilted forward. When he's well, he's indomitable. This is the man who led the Lake Baikal expedition to view the 1887 solar eclipse. In 1890, with Miss Keaton and twenty mixed-race porters trailing, he crossed Chile's Atacama Desert to witness stars coalescing from clouds of gas in the Southern Hemisphere nebulae. This is the man who, when in England, still coxes the crew that regularly defeats Oxford in the annual alumni regatta. This is the man who proposed, first to his stunned astronomical colleagues and then to the world, history's most ambitious scientific endeavor, and the man who endured years of ridicule and calumny for it. This is the man who has brought the project to the verge of completion.

Nevertheless, Miss Keaton knows how to get around him, at least some of the time.

"Then play me! If you win, you'll go. With some men and Dr. McKinnon."

He gazes at her, unsmiling, while he considers the challenge.

"This is foolish, Dee," he says, using his private name for her, an abbreviation for Deimos, the second moon of Mars. Sometimes when they're alone she calls him Pho, for Phobos, its larger companion. "The day's only getting warmer, time is being wasted as we argue," he adds, but he's already removing his helmet and loosening his jacket.

The table occupies its own tent, where it has been unvisited since the day Thayer fell ill. The vellum-lined battledores lie as they were after their last game, in which Miss Keaton defeated the astronomer decisively, twenty points to fifteen. Even after weeks of fever, Thayer certainly recalls the loss, which is why Miss Keaton has suggested a rematch. One of the paddles rests on a small black ball of India rubber.

He takes the far corner, as he always does, and Miss Keaton serves first, as usual and without ceremony. The ball sails past him before he can raise his paddle. He retrieves it and she fires it past him again. He returns the third serve, she puts it into the net, and the game begins in earnest.

Thayer and Miss Keaton rarely declare the score, for they keep close accounts of the game to themselves and there's never a discrepancy. They play quickly, fully absorbed. The ball's thumps against the table are followed by shallower taps as it rises up against the battledores, and in the adjacent offices the clerks look up, arrested by the characteristic, long-absent sounds of the game, relieved that Thayer is playing again. Miss Keaton takes an early lead, forcing him into a defensive posture. His timing's off.

Yet the game tightens and Miss Keaton feels a competitive heat rising within her. The heat is good, something is being ignited. She slams the ball hard into the opposite box, it flies obliquely to Thayer's paddle, and then lands on her side, spinning. The triangle is completed and vanishes into unrecalled geometric space as the black sphere meets her paddle at another point, higher and to her right, drawing the initial line of another figure. Every angle generates its own sines and cosines, calculable relations described by long columns of unseen numbers. Thayer claws his way back to tie the game at seventeen. Moisture beads down her sternum. Before each serve they lock wide, unblinking eyes.

Miss Keaton thoroughly reviles herself when she falls behind on the next point. She will always despise losing, especially against Thayer, who considers himself the much superior player, but today's match is staked. She desperately wants him to remain in camp. Ballard can ride out to see about the rock, if necessary. Yet at the moment Thayer pulls ahead, with the score so close and the decisive point so near, her sentiments flip. It's a peculiar phenomenon, which she's observed in herself before. She feels what he feels: the heat of his grip on the battledore, the pinch of his boots, even the lassitude after the fever against which he's rebelling; she can see her shot approaching him as it barely clears the net and she wants what *he* wants—a point against her, a smash beyond her reach. She knows her empathy is foolishly placed, but the infinitesimal moment of weakness is enough to deflect her next return by a fraction of a degree, just enough to overshoot the table. He presses the advantage and two serves later claims twenty.

"Yah-hah," he says.

"Bugger."

He laughs sharply.

She looks across the table into his cool blue eyes, which, she knows, have charmed women on four continents, not to mention more than one head of state. She detects a certain wateriness there. A gravely faithless notion flits past her, barely making itself known: the wish to see him return to London for proper medical care, the Equilateral be hanged.

Miss Keaton is about to speak, to urge him to reconsider the journey to mile 270, or at least to submit to a rematch, when they realize that another person has joined them inside the tent. They turn. It's Bint. She stands at the tent flap, perfectly still. She's a small girl, not yet fully grown, with plump lips, deep, wide-set eyes under thick brows, and a coarse Semitic nose. She's been there for some time, against the unspoken command within the compound that Thayer and Miss Keaton shouldn't be disturbed during a game. Perhaps she isn't aware of the prohibition. She's puzzled, pondering the meaning of the activity or performance or vital task that she has just witnessed. The secretary wonders if she recognizes it as a game, and whether there's an analogous sport among the Arabs, and whether Arab adults even participate in friendly games and sport. Or does she suppose that this intense effort is somehow connected to the difficult labors being performed on the shifting, searing desert floor?

"Ping-Pong," Thayer explains. "Table tennis."

Bint apprehends the words through the fog of her native

language and tries to return them to him through the same mi-
asma. They come out, "Bong-bong." Miss Keaton detects a small
secret shiver running through the girl's delicate frame.

△

The letter from Hector France-Lanord, the chief astronomer at
Meudon in the Paris suburbs, is accompanied by three fine
sketches in his distinctive charcoal stipple. The French astronomer professes to have seen a new set of parallel shadow lines in
Mare Australe, Mars' dried southern seabed adjacent to the ice
cap. As the two planets glide toward their closest approach,
observers are straining to identify artifacts and natural landforms on the surface that have developed since the previous pas
de deux in 1892. The apparent, or observed, size of the planet's
disk, still only 6.5 seconds of arc, makes its surface features too
small to be distinguished reliably, but Thayer and Miss Keaton,
who respect Meudon's equipment and France-Lanord's eye,
have been intrigued. In six months, on October 12, 1894, the
planets will draw within less than forty million miles of each
other; eight days later Mars will reach opposition, the moment
when it lies directly opposite the Earth from the sun. The Martian disk will swell to 22 seconds and the southern hemisphere
of the planet will be well placed for viewing.

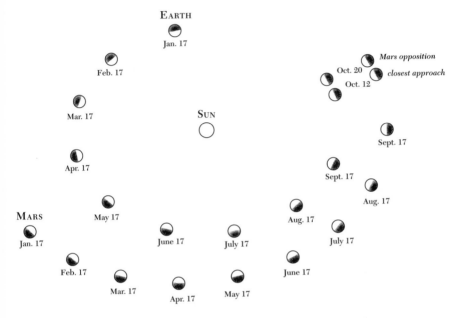

EARTH
Jan. 17
Feb. 17
Mar. 17
SUN
Apr. 17
MARS
Jan. 17
May 17
Feb. 17
June 17
July 17
Mar. 17
Apr. 17
May 17
June 17
Aug. 17
July 17
Aug. 17
Sept. 17
Sept. 17
Oct. 20   *Mars opposition*
Oct. 12   *closest approach*

Earth and Mars, 1894.

SEVEN

As Thayer fears, work has stopped at mile 270. Hundreds of fellahin idly mill in the heat. Some have laid out prayer mats, while others congregate near the water tanker as if it were a seaside refreshment stand. Their spades are sunk in the dirt like a line of pickets. The crates of dynamite brought by the blast crew molder in their wagons. The rock in question, an outcropping hardly fifty feet high, remains unmolested.

Thayer and his men are met by the manager of the blasting crew, a seven-fingered Romanian, or Vlach, who is said to have worked on the St. Gotthard Tunnel. He greets the expedition warmly, praising the miraculously fortunate alignment of stars that have brought them to this site. He inquires whether they would like to stay for dinner. When Thayer demands to know why the rock hasn't been removed, the Romanian says the limestone is a small problem, hardly worth the professor's attention. The rock ends about six hundred yards to the east. The most sensible course of action would be to excavate around it.

"No deviations," Thayer declares, not for the first time.

From the moment the plans for the geometric figure were announced, they've come under assault from those who would subvert them for the convenience of geography. As if the sides of the Equilateral were no more than railroad lines, engineers have proposed skirting outcroppings as well as sand dunes, ridges, gullies, and marshes wherever they encounter them. Thayer has to remind the engineers of the Equilateral's purpose and fundamental principles. If the figure is forced to conform to the Egyptian landscape, the astronomers of Mars will be placed in the same difficult position as their colleagues on Earth: unable to convince parochial skeptics that the markings on the distant planetary surface are the work of sentient beings.

It's the *disregard* of the natural landscape that proves man's intelligence.

Thayer knew of course that there would be topographical obstructions, and for this reason an army of surveyors was mustered to position the Equilateral so that it would fall on the least possible number of them. Yet the foremen protest.

"The removal of this rock will begin within a quarter hour," he declares. "Otherwise I will leave it to you to explain to the men why their pay has been docked."

Thayer and his company, including Dr. McKinnon, remain at mile 270 until the first explosives are set off. Smoke and debris accompany the demolition, yet the force of each blast comes to him diminished, as if muffled by the sands or by the blanket of solar heat, which has gathered its noonday weight. But Thayer is satisfied that the rock is being removed. He gives the signal to return to Point A.

The Romanian, or Vlach (he's actually an Albanian), watches the party leave, pleased with Thayer's inspection. In his anger the astronomer again showed the determination and vigor on which the project depends. News of his illness, which spread quickly among the fellahin up and down Side AC, enervated them and raised the specter of their abandonment in the desert. Thayer's returning vitality will improve morale.

△

Thayer knows that mile 270 is only a single troublesome point on Side AC. Problems have appeared elsewhere. Ballard apparently had to knock heads together last week at mile 64, where a Bedouin work gang encountered some flooding along the marshy area near Nuweimisa. Now the engineer's on his way to Point B, an excursion that will take the better part of a week. Thayer will have to send someone else, one of the junior engineers with a surveyor, to investigate a place on Side BC where two crews, one excavating in a northwesterly direction and the other southeasterly, failed to meet up.

But meanwhile progress has been made on this segment of Side AC, even since the morning. Riding along the side on a high-spirited Arabian, the best in Point A's stables, Thayer peers into the broad trench, where for a mile out thousands of fellahin bow into their labors. Thousands more carry away the debris in hand-barrows. The excavators have been configured into a series of interlocking parallelograms, a geometric system Thayer devised to extract the soil with the greatest efficiency. This afternoon the lines of these figures have unfolded into new territory, extending the side.

The scrape of the spades is accompanied by the men's singing, which ascends like smoke into the incandescent atmosphere. According to a French expert in primitive lyric, the compositions are derived from fragments of existing indigenous airs and have largely replaced them throughout the territories of the Equilateral and beyond. The Equilateral's songs are heard in coffeehouses from Rabat to Baghdad, their tunes strummed on zitherlike qanoons and pear-shaped ouds, or rapped out on darbukkahs. The men sing of their spades easing through the pliant sand and of sand less pliant, and also of their distant homes, as well as of lines and of angles, of triangles acute and obtuse, and of their secants and cosecants, and their rhymes also praise the golden section, in which a line is divided so that the smaller is to the larger as the larger is to the whole; the sagitta, the line that connects the midpoint of an arc to the midpoint of its chord; and the apothem, the line between the center of a polygon and one of its sides, and they give full-throated gratitude to the God who has decreed that the square of the hypotenuse is always equal to the sum of the squares of the sides, making possible the whole of trigonometry and then, lying beneath trigonometry, or around it and above it, the fundamental structure of reality.

Men pause in their labors as Thayer passes by. A few raise their arms; he presumes in salute. They know he has brought them here to win them glory.

EIGHT

The Equilateral *will* be completed and the Flare *will* be ignited June the seventeenth, at one hour, fifty-two minutes, thirty-eight seconds Greenwich time, the instant that lines drawn from the sun to the Earth and from the Earth to Mars meet at a right angle. At that flawless Pythagorean moment, and only for that moment, a right triangle will blaze into existence deep within the heart of the Egyptian desert. The square of Mars's distance from the sun will be equal to the sum of the squares of the distances between the Earth and the sun and the Earth and Mars. The angle at the Earth-Mars-Sun vertex will be 46.9 degrees, the maximum separation between the Earth and the sun as seen from Mars.

With the Concession's funds exhausted, the fellahin will be sent back to their villages. In the autumn the world's telescopes will be swung into position. In these months of painstaking scrutiny, while the Red Planet's disk grows, man will confirm what canals and other artifacts have been constructed since the 1892 approach. Observing the dark blotches of vegetation that appear every Martian spring in the vicinity of the planet's irrigation projects, terrestrial astronomers will count the victories

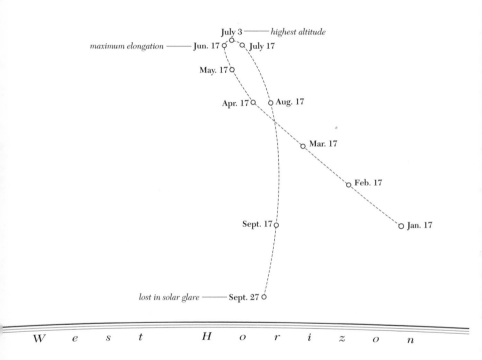

July 3 ———— highest altitude

maximum elongation ——— Jun. 17

July 17

May. 17

Apr. 17

Aug. 17

Mar. 17

Feb. 17

Sept. 17

Jan. 17

lost in solar glare ——— Sept. 27

W e s t H o r i z o n

**Earth as seen from Mars, 1894,
end of evening twilight.**

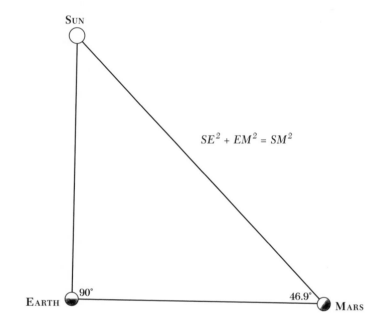

Earth at maximum elongation, June 17, 1894.

their neighbors have won and the losses they have suffered in their struggle for survival. The astronomers will search too for some acknowledgment that the planet's inhabitants have received the signal from Earth and are aware that intelligent beings share the solar system.

Earth will leave it to Mars, an older planet whose civilization must be superior in technology, morals, and interplanetary manners, to frame a proper response to the Equilateral. Thayer speculates that its inhabitants will fire back a Flare of their own, or that some geometry-based heliographic system may be deployed, or that Mars will perform its own symbolic excavations. Earth will be obliged to respond in kind, with every device at its disposal.

Thayer does not envision that his work will be completed June 17, 1894. More digging will have to be done, even if there is no immediate signal in return from Mars. In the ensuing two years, once the funds are raised, a new 266-mile line will be excavated in the Western Desert, from Point C to the midpoint of Side AB, which will be designated Point D. This bisection of the Equilateral, creating two Right Triangles, will be completed in time for the 1896 approach.

These excavations will prepare the desert ground for the next great Figure: a Circle tangent to Lines AD and CD at Points F and G, with its locus, Point E, near the Twenty-seventh Parallel, in time for maximum elongation in 1898. The Circle's diameter will be equal to each of the Equilateral's sides, casting a circumference of 968 miles whose arc will cross the frontier with Tripoli, still a Turkish dominion but increasingly within the shadow of Italian ambitions to secure a foothold in

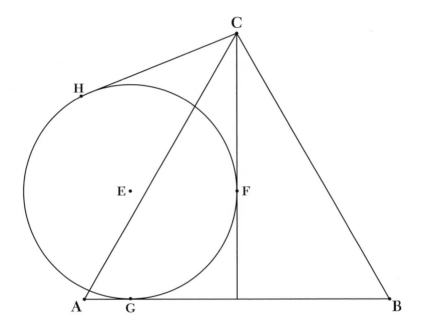

Further excavations.

North Africa. Certain diplomatic maneuvers will have to be accomplished. Another tangent, from Point C to Point H, can be foreseen.

By then Thayer will have begun constructing with Mars a common language based on the two planets' shared knowledge of trigonometry, its words, its grammar, and its syntax flowing from the fixed relations between the length and positions of the Equilateral's line segments, their angles of incidence, and the universal trigonometric concepts that can be derived from them. By constructing each side of the Equilateral 306.928 miles in length, precisely 1/73rd of the Earth's circumference at the figure's base, Thayer has brought a prime number, 73, into the conversation. Mars will recognize its significance: the ratio of Side AB to the Earth's circumference will be prime in whatever counting system is favored by the fourth planet. By making AB parallel to the Earth's equator and Line CD parallel to its axis of rotation, Thayer confirms man's knowledge of his planet's motion, which depends on other quantities that Mars could independently verify. These are the terms by which the solar system's two species of intelligence will first begin to know each other.

Thayer hunches over his inclined drafting table, plotting the position of the planets when the 1900 and 1901 approach will occur. He requires few tools, for the complicated paths celestial objects appear to take across the curved firmament overhead—the pirouettes, the variable rising and setting times, the lunar and planetary phases, the sun's long summer days and long winter absences—derive from simple clockwork motions within the three dimensions of transparent space, as perfect and predictable and omnipotent as any geometry. While he steadies a compass around one of the foci of the Martian orbital ellipse, his pencil rolls off the table and drops soundlessly onto the Persian rug beneath the table.

"Bint!"

The girl appears beside him at once. She has probably been here all this time.

"Would you be so kind as to hand me the pencil?"

The girl doesn't stir.

"The pencil, Bint?" Thayer says, and he recalls, as he must several times a day, that the girl speaks no English. Daoud Pasha offered to replace her with one who does, but Thayer has never accepted or rejected the proposal, not even making a gesture to indicate his indifference. Now, with his hands still on the compass, he dips his head toward the carpet and asks for the pencil again.

She doesn't follow the movement of his head. He looks into her eyes and then down at the pencil, then back at the warm deep pools of her eyes and again at the pencil. When he returns to her face, she's still looking directly into his. She offers the faintest, most respectful suggestion of amusement. Perhaps it's there, perhaps it's not.

Thayer laughs despite his frustration. He puts down the compass and goes to his knees. He'll have to redraw the diagram from scratch.

"Pencil," he says, holding it up to her face. "Pencil."

Perhaps she has now learned the word for pencil. Or perhaps she believes she's learned the word for raising an object before someone's face, or the word for the color of the pencil, which is in fact vermilion, or the word for recovering an object that has fallen, or the word for the flush that the exertion has brought to Thayer's temples, or the word for laughing in frustration. She doesn't repeat the word.

But she holds his stare. He studies her face with the idea that he will see it for the first time. He doesn't succeed. Something veils her aspect, a cloud or a shadow.

NINE

Thayer's health continues to improve, but Miss Keaton keeps her office near his quarters. Through one of the dragomen, she instructs Bint that he must take his quinine without fail.

Having returned from Point B, Ballard sourly notes the secretary's protectiveness, which reminds him why he doesn't like having ladies involved in engineering projects. Even when they don't interfere directly in the endeavor, they project their fears and weaknesses onto their men. Thayer will benefit from an evening without Miss Keaton's company.

Ballard suggests that he join him after dinner. A severely water-rationed hammam has been established on the far side of the encampment, hard by the diggers' quarters, within a complex of mud-brick structures that tend to the laborers' necessities, including their basest. Parallel facilities for white men lie adjacent and include a tea room that serves as the Club, some of whose furnishings Ballard has seen to himself: Anatolian kilims, water pipes, and a Bedouin saddle hung on the wall alongside an antique astrolabe. The engineer knows the astronomer usually enjoys an evening among men, whether they're the world's most distinguished astronomers or, at Point A, the Equilateral's engineers and overseers, some of whom have been under Ballard for decades and took heroic part in the construction of the great new barrage-dam at Aswan.

When they arrive at the tea room, Ballard and Thayer receive respectful, if wary, acknowledgments from the men, followed by a deep bow from the proprietor, Daoud Pasha. The Turk serves the new guests himself, attentive to information or any gesture or sign that he might turn to profit. Besides tending to the hammam and the tea room, Daoud Pasha has his hand in most of the Equilateral's provisioning, under arrangements that remain obscure.

Ballard thinks the astronomer's health has been compromised by too many nights in his tent with his astronomical charts and tables. His solicitations are sincerely tendered, but he also knows that his friend's fatigue and pallor threaten the project's completion as much as the marshes on Side AC do. The lavish expenditures of capital, the stupendous tonnage of machinery hauled to this wasteland, and the exhaustive outlay of physical effort dedicated to the excavations depend on immaterial theory and desire: Thayer's. The Concession's real investment lies primarily in the flesh-and-blood astronomer. Keeping him whole is the chief engineer's responsibility, no less than it is Miss Keaton's.

Thayer in turn likes Ballard but suspects that for him the Equilateral is no more than another civil engineering project and, preoccupied with the impediments, he fails to regard its grandeur. Ballard is an unreflective man. His decades in the desert haven't left him with much of an affinity for quietude—he smokes, but not for him the contemplative drag on the hookah.

KEN KALFUS

Now he leans over his tumbler of gin, about to make a point. He's had too much to drink already. Thayer wonders whether, in a life under cloudless night skies, Ballard has ever thought about the stars and their secrets. As they led him across the burning sands of the Empty Quarter, did he listen to their murmurings? Did he dwell on their hidden and contradictory desires? Thayer is baffled that for modern men astronomy has lost its ancient status as the principal art, on which depend all other occupations, including engineering. Those who raised the pyramids knew the stars and kept in their good graces.

Yet Ballard has succeeded in driving the project forward, when the most renowned engineers of his age were intimidated by its ambitions. Sir John Hawkshaw declared that without a railroad it would be impossible to transport the necessary equipment into the Western Desert. István Türr predicted that windblown sands would obscure the figure long before it was completed. Ferdinand de Lesseps, Le Grand Français, the Builder of Suez, announced that the Equilateral could not be accomplished, neither for twice the price nor with five times the number of laborers. The single task of keeping nine hundred thousand men alive in the Western Desert, bringing them their every swallow of water and morsel of food, had daunted the greatest military men of the world's greatest powers. Ballard has shown them that it can be done. Thayer recognizes that history will regard the Equilateral as much Ballard's achievement as his own.

Now the engineer declares, "Sanford, I've heard rumors of war. It was a blunder to stop at the Atbara River, thank Whitehall, but reinforcements are on the way. Warwicks and the

Cameron Highlanders. Surely this year's campaign will strike directly at Omdurman. The khalif will be ground into dust, don't you think?"

"I suppose," Thayer says vaguely. Fatigued by his illness, he's drinking only tea tonight. "I haven't seen the newspapers."

"This isn't in the newspapers," Ballard says, further deepening the creases around his sun-damaged eyes. "This is confidential information, the troops have been seen disembarking in Alexandria, and it has some bearing on our enterprise. The troops are welcome, if the reports are true, for there's not a single regiment between us and the Sudan. I don't think you'd fancy having a thousand of those dervish boys showing up in camp tomorrow."

"No, I wouldn't," Thayer concedes. "Not unless they come with spades."

Ballard's nod is grim. They had come with rifles to the Aswan Barrage—antiques, no match for the Maxims, but still, it was a nasty business, horses and men dead in the Nile, so bloated in the heat they could barely be distinguished from each other. Ballard has no Maxims here.

△

In the concluding decade of the nineteenth century, Egypt is a land where political power rests on semiviscous sands. The long-dying Ottoman Empire's suzerainty has given way to British occupation. While the British consul general, Lord Cromer, exercises his nation's control of Suez and the shipping lanes to India, just beyond Egypt's borders the Sudan remains unsettled, under the sway of fanatics devoted to the Messiah they call the Mahdi. For years the Mahdists have been making trouble, but now rifles have been brought into play and railroads and telegraphs have hastened the spread of religious infection. Europeans in Khartoum face brazen harassment. Raiders from the rebel capital, Omdurman, cross the Twenty-second Parallel without impediment. The savage beheading of General Charles Gordon and the destruction of his troops, sent to Khartoum to restore order, still aggrieves civilized sentiment nine years later.

In feverish, corrupt Cairo, the Khedive Abbas Hilmy II, technically an Ottoman viceroy, maintains a palace and an army under Lord Cromer's supervision. He has granted the Mars Concession in exchange for certain material considerations and in the private belief that Egypt's destiny enfolds the Equilateral. At dusk the military-trained son of Tewfik and the great-great-grandson of Mehmet Ali, the first khedive, steps from his palace chambers onto a marbled terrace and gazes upon the distant Platonic solids in Gizeh, their stones as soft as halvah in the guttering light. The strength and ambition of youth run in his blood on these melancholy evenings; he also senses, coursing through him, his people's millennia, majestic and submissive, enigmatic and frequently catastrophic.

TEN

The brothel operates invisibly, though its presence is as palpable as the chill of the desert night. Thayer knows the brothel, the bagnio, is here, even if he's ignorant of its precise location within the encampment. The girls are never witnessed outside its doors, neither in the dining halls nor within the labyrinth of paths and alleys that emanate from Vertex BAC. Smoking with Ballard, who can't help vexing them both with talk of war and politics, Thayer believes that he hears a sigh, or a grunt, or a rustle behind the fabric of things, but these sounds can easily have been made by Daoud Pasha, who stares into space while he cleans a glass or pipestem. Thayer listens deeply, trying to gain information from these whispers, yet the brothel remains no more than a speculation. In the darkness we speculate. From the darkness we draw hypotheses that conform less to observation than they do to our needs, especially our need for companionship. We presume every desire is complemented by its object, somewhere.

But eventually, as the night deepens, Thayer's observations are confirmed and the hypothesis is proven.

The engineer stands abruptly and hitches his trousers. He

returns his glass to the table with force, as if unsure that it will stay there. When he winks he betrays uncharacteristic embarrassment. His face colors. Without another word he strides off through a canvas flap, opposite the tea room's entrance. A few moments later Thayer hears a girl's bright, explosive laugh.

Other girls dwell in the shadows beyond, scores of them within the dormitory located a few hundred yards away, one of Point A's few buildings constructed of stone, at Miss Keaton's insistence. The Equilateral's labor force is overwhelmingly male, but women have been brought to the points to do char work and serve in the infirmaries. Bint presumably retires there when she's not caring for Thayer. The entrance to the residence hall is protected by a detachment of Nubian guards, who regularly draw on the honor they are meant to protect. In any event these unchaperoned, unmarried females will be considered no less ruined than their sisters in the bagnio once the Equilateral is completed and they are sent back to their villages.

Sipping the tea, which has gone cold, and touched by a corresponding chill in the small of his back, Thayer anticipates the return of his fever. Ballard's departure has taken the last of his vitality with him. In return the engineer has left Thayer the dervishes. The dervishes are known to infiltrate themselves among the fellahin, watching, waiting, striking once our guard is down. The dervishes will slit our throats and then vanish into the night, leaving no tracks in the sand. Thayer has never met or spoken with a dervish, nor, for certain, seen a dervish, but their existence has been conclusively established.

He must have fallen asleep because his next moment of awareness comes abruptly, threatening stark revelation, even though the hand that touches his shoulder is a gentle one.

"Effendi."

It's Bint. Framed in a white headdress, her face is small, dark, and oval. Her eyes dart nervously like little birds. Daoud Pasha stands behind her, showing concern, yet his lips curl. He has learned one or two things in the last few hours.

"She will take you back to your apartments, sir."

Bint has been dispatched by Miss Keaton, who, as a lady, would not be welcome in the tea room. Miss Keaton will later ask herself if she has cause to regret this expedient.

Now the astronomer suspects that he's smoked hashish in the pipe with Ballard; when he tries to stand his lower body gives way. He leans against Bint. She's a slight, almost frail girl, but she takes his weight without complaint. The body beneath the folds of her gown is warm, soft, and pliant. The two stagger from the tea room, past the fellahin waiting near the entrance to the hammam. The men turn away as they leave, as if to deny seeing Thayer impaired.

Thayer and the girl move forward several hundred feet and the lights and sounds of the hammam recede. Thayer is gradually refreshed by the night air, making him even more aware of an excitement that has begun to churn through his clotted being, radiating from Bint's touch. The time in the tea room, with its talk of troops and dervishes, evaporates as quickly as a desert puddle. Although he's aware that their closeness has already come up against the borders of propriety, he doesn't pull away.

The stars are out, as they've been every night for the past

two years and in the hushed ages before them, dependably in their places as the seasons rotated through the crystal empyrean. Now it's the month of April, well into the night. The Great Bear has begun to lumber beneath the horizon, making way for the Virgin and the lush lactic wash of the Milky Way. The planets tumble through their epicycles. The moon has already set. That makes it just past three. The seeing is excellent, eight or nine of ten on the Douglass Scale, marred only by some shifting currents in the upper atmosphere. Nights like these always intoxicate him with their possibility. Half the universe hangs above the desert floor, each star its own sun, each sun circled by worlds composed of the same elements that animate matter on Earth. The sky may be as alive as a deep warm pond in a sunny glade.

In the east the luminous star in Aquila draws his attention. He lifts his arm to it.

"That is Alpha Aquilae," he says. "Otherwise known as Altair."

He's surprised when this provokes an open smile, as strong an expression of Bint's sentiments as he's ever witnessed. As she puts his things in order or brings him his meals, her gestures are more likely to be demure and self-contained. She tends to hover into visibility and then, before he can establish her presence, she vanishes. Now she repeats the star's name, casting it with a foreign inflection, "Al-*tair*."

"That's originally Arabic," Thayer concedes. "Altair, 'the flying eagle.' Or vulture."

"*Al-nasr al-tair*," she declares. This is the star's full appellation, in Arabic. She raises her arm abruptly and points not far from Altair, to an even brighter star. "Wega," she says.

Bint speaks so rarely that the sound of her voice is like the disclosure of a secret. The syllables emerge softly and resonant. He gazes with her at the second star, white with a touch of sapphire, so radiant they can almost be warmed by it.

"Vega," he confirms. "So you know some of the sky."

She extends a long finger with clipped, unvarnished nails at another blue-white first-magnitude star, about twenty degrees from Vega. It's the most prominent object in Cygnus and also commands an ancient name that has survived intact its passage through the Greek and Latin cosmologies. "Deneb," she says.

How many Arab girls in camp, or fellahin in the work crews dozing tonight alongside their excavations, can identify the vertices of the conspicuous, nearly equilateral triangle, Altair-Vega-Deneb, that dominates the Northern Hemisphere's sky on spring mornings and summer evenings? For the most part they never look upward, their attention fixed on the immediate and the mundane, the terrestrial.

"That's right, Bint. Very good."

Grinning now, he shows her the pale yellow light in the southwest, burning steadily close to Spica. This is a trick. It's not a fixed star.

Thayer says, "Saturn. The planet Saturn."

Bint repeats, "Saturn." She hesitates for several moments before she adds, "Zuhal."

He's astounded. "Zuhal?" He didn't know the Arabic name for the planet.

She smiles back, shyly. His sudden attention is intimidating. Thayer rarely has occasion to look at the girl directly. "Zuhal," she asserts.

Saturn: one of the torrid giants like Jupiter, still solidifying into planetary form, a vast seething cauldron of vapors, impossibly hostile to life. But as the spheres cool over the next hundreds of thousands or millions of years, according to the principles of planetary evolution as laid out by Kant and Laplace, and then developed by Chamberlain and refined by Thayer, each sufficiently large planet will get its turn. The evolution of worlds is no less inevitable than the evolution of the species inhabited by them, followed by the evolution of those species' intelligences.

Thayer and Bint continue several yards toward his compound and then stop. He turns due east and looks across the wastes to a point just above the Egyptian horizon, past the temples at Luxor and the Mohammedan's holiest places. The night has gone cold. Some fine grains are swirling up from the Sudan. He softly touches her arm.

They both see it rising, our most beguiling planetary neighbor, red like a pomegranate seed, red like a blood spot on an egg, red like a ladybug, red like a ruby or more specifically a red beryl, red like coral, red like an unripe cherry, red like a Hindu lady's bindi, red like the eye of a nocturnal predator, red like a fire on a distant shore, the subject of his every dream and his every scientific pursuit.

"Mars," he says.

"Merrikh," she tells him.

He repeats after her: "Merrikh."

He admires the sound of it, biblical and arid and altogether strange. *Merrikh.*

She says the word again, emphasizing the final voiceless velar fricative, so favored in the East.

"Merrikh," he says, indicating the planet again, and then he points to the ground. "Earth."

She says, "Masr." Masr is the Arabic word for Egypt. She pronounces it with a Bedouin drawl.

He corrects her gently. "Earth."

"*Urrth, Masr. Masr, Urrth.*" She smiles again, believing that she's learned another word of English.

Perhaps if Thayer knew the Arabic name for our planet he would set her right. But he doesn't know it and the thought occurs to him that a separate word for Earth, analogous to other planetary names, presumes an awareness that Earth, Mars, and Saturn are analogous entities, similar spheres similarly hurtling through the same celestial environment, an airless, matterless medium known as "space." It also presumes an awareness that other political and national entities have been established on Earth, apart from Egypt.

△

There's too much to presume or explain. He doesn't know what she knows, he can't. He allows her to take him to his quarters, a faint glow five hundred yards farther. They walk without speaking, several feet apart now despite the fallen temperature, keenly sensible that their footfalls in the soft sand are weightless.

The lamp is lit in his secretary's bureau. He frowns briefly before he opens the door.

"You needn't have waited up, Dee! I appear to be in good hands."

Miss Keaton is fully dressed and at her desk, schematics of the pipeline equipment laid out around her. She's been contemplating a new difficulty. In a diplomatic maneuver to share the Concession's contracts across national borders, the manufacture of the thirty-inch cylinders that will carry the petroleum to the taps along the Sides has been allocated to individual companies in Germany, Belgium, and France, while the two-ton brass taps come from Britain—and each has apparently manufactured them to slightly different specifications. A supply of Belgian pipes that arrived at Point C last week is proving to be entirely unusable. She sits back in her chair now, smiling wanly at Thayer and Bint.

"Sanford, if you fall ill again . . ."

She had observed his pallor when he left with Ballard. She now distrusts the animation with which he has announced his return from the hammam.

"The girl knows the sky! It's extraordinary, I doubt she reads a word, but she can identify the stars and planets. I should test her on the constellations."

"It's late!"

"Yes, it is, past three. Mars is already over the horizon. It'll be well placed by the time we open the shed."

She calculates what has transpired. The girl's eyes luster against the hour and some color has been raised upon her dusky cheeks, certainly brought there by Thayer's courtly attentions. She's not even pretty, not by any familiar measure, but Miss Keaton can never guess which female from the lower classes, which serving girl or scullery maid or artist's model, will next draw the astronomer's gaze.

Thayer says, "Think of it, she's never looked through a telescope."

It's been weeks since Thayer has. Miss Keaton understands, however, that he will allow no mention of his illness. Also, that they are not yet done with the night.

△

They leave the office, Bint following them several hundred yards down a smooth, swept sidewalk, one of the first fixtures of civilization introduced to Point A two years before. It leads directly into the desert, where, at the end of the path, stands a twelve-sided clapboard structure with a conical, shuttered roof. The door to the building is locked. Only Thayer and Miss Keaton have the keys. Every time they unlock the door they're relieved to discover that the nine-inch refracting telescope, built by Alvan Clark & Sons of Boston, is still there, neither blown away nor dematerialized by the *khamsin*, nor carried off by the dervishes.

The dervishes would have had to dismantle the ninety-six-inch light green steel tube, which stands on a cast-iron pier, and all its accessories. With the equatorial mount and clock drive that compensate for the stars' relentless whirl around the axis of the earth, the telescope weighs eleven hundred pounds. Thayer and Miss Keaton themselves have dismantled it, knowing its every mechanical intricacy, taking it apart and putting it together several times in several distant lands. With a single practiced motion, the astronomer now pulls on a lever below the rail on which the roof sits and half the shutters slide away to open the instrument to the sky.

Saturn lingers above the horizon in the west, its rings beyond the capacity to imagine for someone who hasn't already seen their pictures in a book, a fantastic confection, a miracle, but he doesn't make Bint the gift. He sweeps the telescope across the sky to the Red Planet, which is just now cresting over the shed's eastern wall. Running a closer, faster track around the sun, the Earth is gaining on Mars, so that every morning the planet rises several minutes earlier than the morning before, preceding the stars with which it sojourned the previous night.

Mars! The mythmakers have associated it with armed conflict, poets have sung of it, and, finally, in this century, astronomers have identified the sphere as home to living organisms, the solar system's only other world known to be inhabited, a world with bodies of water and an atmosphere. Astronomers have recognized seasonal variations in its flora. They've observed the artifacts under construction by Martian intelligence. Now, as it crosses Capricornus night by night toward Aquarius, the planet fairly pulses, fairly breathes, fairly glowers with life. Yet it presents a featureless, dimensionless crimson disk when Thayer first slides it into the view of the eyepiece, which projects from the bottom of the tube. Patience is required. The eye must accustom itself. Light pools on the retina, building an image in the brain. The disk is still tiny, a single carat on a bed of velvet even when enlarged 450 times, as high a magnification as the Clark's objective lens makes practical.

And still Mars withholds its charms. The disk remains empty of meaning. At the time of the solar system's murky origins and in accordance with the unforgiving equations of celestial mechanics, the planet was inserted into an orbit just a few million miles beyond the range of man's best, most confident scrutiny. It will always beckon him, tantalize him, seduce him, and then remain chaste to his advances, before dancing out of sight into the void.

"The wind's picked up," Miss Keaton remarks.

Thayer adjusts his chair to bring it closer to the eyepiece. The seeing has been degraded. There's an extra twinkle in the stars.

Hoping to find at least one familiar Martian feature, Thayer fixes his study on the southernmost edge of the planet, at the upper part of the inverted image. It's early spring in the southern hemisphere. Very gradually over several silent, motionless minutes, the glare subsides. First the polar cap becomes visible, pale against the disk, extending to about sixty-five degrees south latitude.

Then, before he's fully conscious of it, he discerns something stirring on the surface of the planet; no, it's beneath the surface, bubbling up. Vague ripples. Shadows. Shadows of shadows. They're there and then they're gone and then they're back, more emphatically. The lines shudder before they take the positions where he knows they will be, according to the maps he has drawn himself. The canals. Deeper he looks into the disk and he's rewarded, for a moment, by a glimpse of the thin gray lines horizontally traversing the circular, elevated Hellas region. This is Peneus, the waterway named after the great river whose waters were employed by Hercules to flush the Augean stables. The vernal melting of the southern ice cap has likely filled the south-central canals, irrigating the adjacent land. This area at the edge of Mare Australe pullulates with the spring crops, whatever strange vegetable matter they may be.

Thayer teases out the outline of Mare Australe. It's just more than a month since France-Lanord reported developments in the southern hemisphere.

"Shadowing? Possibly, I'm not sure they're new," Thayer murmurs after several minutes, his face still at the eyepiece. For years Thayer and Miss Keaton have spoken to each other in these postures, one stooped at the instrument, the other a few steps back, watching, never looking face-to-face, while they shared their most important observations. "He believes it's around Peneus."

"Yes."

"Yes," he echoes. After a long while he says, "Damn. Damn the air."

"Pho."

"Ah, hold on," he says. Below the sea, broken in places, lies some kind of new strip or stripe. "Something's there, I think." A thready line appears to emanate from Agyre, at the edge of the dead sea—perhaps the vanguard of a waterway project, now that he considers it in the light of France-Lanord's sketches. Other astronomers who have received the French sketches are also looking hard at the region tonight, seeking to detect a shadow, a discoloration, a figment at the limit of perception on the surface of an object that remains 130 million miles from Earth. Astronomers will study their drawings from previous oppositions. Photographs were taken at the 1892 approach, but their large-grained emulsions, the only ones available, were insufficiently sensitive to reveal what may be apprehended by the human eye. Not a single canal has ever been distinguished in a photograph.

Thayer looks for several minutes and makes a careful sketch in his notebook before he pulls away. "Have a look yourself."

"Let the poor girl look. She's shivering."

Thayer has already forgotten Bint, who's standing apart from the astronomer and his secretary. She's wrapped her robe tight against her frame, but it's hardly enough to keep out the sands' early morning chill.

Thayer raises his hand and shows Bint the eyepiece.

"Merrikh," he says.

She takes small steps as she approaches the instrument. Thayer wonders whether she comprehends the telescope's purpose; whether she will make the connection between the image in the eyepiece and the steady red beacon low above the horizon. She's small enough to stand erect at the eyepiece. She does as Thayer did, opening her right eye wide to the lens, a few sixteenths of an inch above it. She's motionless as she demonstrates the native patience that has been won from the desert's silence.

"Look well, Bint," Thayer instructs her. "Look hard. Everything worth seeing lies at the edge of visibility."

Miss Keaton murmurs her assent. This was one of the first lessons Thayer gave her, years ago, when she first came into his employ.

He adds, "Every discovery lies within the standard error of measurement. The most important truths about the cosmos can hardly be separated from illusion."

"She can't understand you, Sanford."

Offered a view through a telescope, most lay observers look briefly, presuming they have seen what they were supposed to. But Bint remains at the eyepiece for minutes, as if in fact she's directly executing his command. Waiting her turn, Miss Keaton believes she can pick out the reflection of the planet's image on the surface of the girl's eye. She thinks she may even see in this mirroring the creamy tip of the ice cap. Thayer also watches Bint attentively, expectantly. He too perceives the sanguine glint. Bint's moist, budlike lips are parted as she gazes into the eyepiece. Miss Keaton reconsiders. The girl is slender and submissive, her skin is clear, and the very crudeness of her features impart an almost classical sensuality. Thayer could conceivably consider her attractive.

"Merrikh," the girl repeats, murmuring.

She continues to ignore Thayer and Miss Keaton. Her only motion is a small, peculiar one: the light, absentminded passage of a finger from her right hand across the palm of her left.

When she finally draws away from the telescope she turns to Thayer, smiling openly, in a womanly way, without the deference that he should expect. He doesn't mind. She holds out her palm and traces a circle on it with a fingernail. Once that's complete she draws another line across her hand, where the memory of the circle is imprinted. If the circle represents Mars, then the line's termini may very possibly approximate the positions of Peneus and the arid patch of Martian ground known as Agyre.

"You've seen something?" Thayer's eyes light. "You've seen definite features!"

Miss Keaton knows that Bint's recognition of the new artifact is extraordinary. The first time laypeople observe the planet through a telescope they rarely see any landforms at all, not even the ice caps. Their impatience makes it difficult to convince skeptics of the canals' reality: *"I didn't see them, so they can't be there!"* One would not then expect the ready detection of surface features by an unlettered Bedouin serving girl. Her confirmation of the shadowing gives substantial credence to the French astronomer's claim. France-Lanord will have to be cabled in the morning, which is almost upon them.

Bint gives up her place to the secretary, who's at first presented with the usual blank crimson disk. Regardless of her long experience with the instrument, she too is obliged to wait for her eyes to adapt. Miss Keaton's aware that in these several minutes, Thayer and Bint are in the position of having seen something that she has not. They stand behind her, waiting. Soon, though, the image appears, starting at the ice cap, an even gray line, something that wasn't there during the 1892 approach. The new canal can only confirm that the inhabitants of Mars remain capable of grand construction. Their race is still a worthy audience for the spectacle of the Equilateral. But a disquiet tugs at her. Something she can't quite make out.

ELEVEN

The secretary requires the remaining hours before dawn to complete the report, which she signs with Thayer's name, adding that the observation was joined by Miss A. Keaton. The second witness provides superfluous confirmation, for Thayer's visual powers are unrivaled among his peers—he's identified incipient squalls in the atmosphere of the sun before they became raging cyclones the size of the Earth; he's mapped Himalayan peaks on the surface of Jupiter's Ganymede—but the astronomer routinely asks her to share priority.

The morning has not yet warmed when she steps from her tent on the way to the telegraphic bureau, the carefully typed paper in hand. The camp is still waking, and there's still no birdsong. The embers of last night's cooking fires are being stirred and reanimated. Men make their stiff-legged way toward the latrines. A fellahin work gang lingers in the distance, before departing for labors to be performed on Side AC. An unseen muezzin clears his throat, about to launch into the day's first devotions.

Miss Keaton's strides across the packed sands are long and confident, whatever uncertainty from the night having dissipated with the night itself. She sees men falling to the ground. The repeated cries in the muezzin's first line reach her now: *Allahu Akbar! Allahu Akbar! Allahu Akbar! Allahu Akbar!* They're a kind of comfort and a kind of thrill. She reflects on how awful the song would seem to the women who were her school friends a decade earlier, girls who were bright, sophisticated, and daring—every one of them now married into anonymity. None would care to imagine herself under this sun, treading these wastes, and sharing this remote camp with thousands of men, or that Adele would possibly consider herself anything but unfortunate.

The night telegraph man is still on duty, another Turk with a tarbush, or perhaps it's the same Turk from the water bureau. He rises from his prayer rug. When she hands him the report, he bows with possibly exaggerated courtesy. She stands away, looking out on the sands while he tap-tap-taps the message to Europe. The mechanism produces another repetitive sound, no less all-encompassing than the muezzin's prayers. The transmission concludes with her name reduced to a series of dots and dashes and reassembled thousands of miles away, with harm neither to her person nor to her reputation. At this moment, she herself takes in the distance between Point A and London, over desert and sea. By some similar magic or technology, she may yet someday span the vacancy between Point A and the planet Mars.

TWELVE

Thayer, Ballard, and several junior engineers ride out to mile 50 on Side AB, where there's a segment of the triangle that hasn't been reached by the work crews. The astronomer is perplexed. They were scheduled to complete it months before. This is some of the easiest territory they will have to cut through, the ground soft and unobstructed, almost begging to be excavated.

Having dismounted, Thayer steps away from his party, engineers who can enumerate unequivocally the reasons this section has yet to see a spade or hand-barrow. He feels a rising disgust for the men's company. Once he turns, he's the last person on Earth, the last of everything. No living creature respires within his field of view, which extends hundreds of miles. His boots kick through some chalky sand that embed a reflection of the geometric design in their soles, a series of equilateral triangles. Thayer squats to run a hand through the loose dirt.

He picks up several small flat round stones about an inch wide, each stamped with the fanlike image of a brachiopod that is no longer represented among the Earth's extant species. A dozen such stones lie in the immediate area a few yards between him and the engineers, rebuking the numbskulls and scoundrels who deny the evidence for evolution by natural selection.

Thayer stands on land that was once the bottom of a shallow Saharan sea, in an epoch long before the supposed flood of Noah, but one that was just as wet, when the Earth was primarily an aqueous planet. Whales, dolphins, and fish plied the waters, nesting in future wadis and savoring the fresh, cooling streams that rose from the future oases. They were content in their dominions, unaware that evolution conspired against them. Then the waters receded, leaving sand and their fossilized remains, and providing for the emergence of another species, one that would establish his home on land and from that redoubt rule the planet.

The closing century has succeeded in proving what previous times have only fitfully suggested: that history moves in a single direction and that the direction is forward. Since 1800, railroads have replaced horse-drawn conveyances, photography has replaced the inexact daubings of painters, and representative legislatures have replaced despots. These innovations have dramatically enlarged man's imagination. Charles Darwin's theories have won acceptance precisely because the evolution of living species echoes the progress of our age.

Thayer has offered his own contributions to the idea, advanced most prominently by the philosopher Herbert Spencer, that evolution is a universal process that governs the development of inanimate matter as well as it does Earth's species of life and the progress of human societies. We may confirm this principle by simply lifting our heads to the sky, where gas and dust are constantly evolving into more complex celestial objects. In his pioneering 1890 expedition to Chile, Thayer observed diffuse entities visible from the Southern Hemisphere, particularly the Large and Small Magellanic Clouds. According to settled nineteenth century opinion, these nebulae are relatively close by, located within a Milky Way that comprises the entire universe. Thayer's observations have shown that they're individual stars precipitating from incandescent gas before our very eyes, dust and gas evolving into stars and planets, a process that eventually casts our individual human destinies—a process that at this moment in our planetary history *demands* the Equilateral.

The logic of the excavations is drawn from confirmed theory.

Like Darwin's species, the planets gain new attributes and lose others depending on conditions in their environment. Astronomers will catalogue these characteristics sometime in the next century, but one lesson that has already been learned, from observation through this century's best instruments, is that it's in the nature of planets to lose their water as they age. The Earth and its closest neighbors provide striking illustrations of the principle. The youngest of the three, oceanic Venus, is shrouded by clouds and most likely lacks a single island of dry land from one pole to the other. As may be seen through even a small telescope, Mars between the ice caps is almost totally waterless, on the verge of extinction. Our home planet Earth, older than the second sphere from the sun but more youthful than the fourth, is delicately poised in what Thayer calls the terraqueous stage, its surface contested by vast seas and immense continents.

If life typically rises from a planet's aquatic depths, then Venus most likely hosts primitive organisms similar to the algae and plankton that dominated Cambrian Earth. Mars is then home to the most evolutionarily developed fauna, capable of adapting to its harsh, arid climate.

These considerations imply that the driest of the three planets, Mars, should boast the oldest, most storied, most advanced civilization. As the construction of its planet-girdling canals demonstrates, Mars has progressed far beyond mankind in the sciences and in technology. If men have operated steam engines for two hundred years, the engineers of Mars have employed them for two hundred thousand, continuously making refinements. They may have raised towers that reach the edges of the planet's attenuated atmosphere; they may have perfected airships and other vehicles, railed or not, that can cross the ruddy globe in hours. As we can observe, they've developed agricultural techniques that produce bountiful crops in lands far more desiccated than the Western Desert.

We may observe that morals are another trait subject to the forces of evolution. Human history shows that ethical practices ensuring a race's survival and well-being are naturally promoted, while malign behaviors are inexorably discarded. In the course of Earth's past two thousand years the principles of right and wrong have been bred into the Anglo-Saxon races, which have come to dominate the planet. In their native lands contracts are honored in letter and spirit. Girls grow into ladies with innate modesty, blessed by the sanctity of marriage. The Golden Rule has triumphed on both sides of the Atlantic. So has industry, sobriety, and self-possession.

Mars is home to a race in which the forces of natural selection have enjoyed further millennia to secure positive social traits. To judge from the planetary cooperation that must have been required to build the canal network, selflessness is imbued deeply within the Martian character. We may imagine then that Martian ethics, the product of many centuries' further wisdom, reflection, and natural selection, have far exceeded our own—though those scruples can't be identified in advance by the most refined, kindest man on Earth, trapped in his own species' intermediate stage of moral development.

Thayer asserts that when we behold Mars, we're witnessing the manifestation of Darwin's theories on the grandest planetary scale. In demonstrating that Earth's terraqueous state is but a phase of planetary evolution, Mars permits us a vision of our own future, existential and moral. Our planet too is destined to lose its oceans and great lakes. Earth's orbit runs closer to the sun, so our sphere will become even hotter and drier than Mars. The deserts will spread like an infection, until water becomes as precious for us as it is for our neighbors. What will civilized man do in that event? Following the Arab's example, he may fall into dissolution, unable to survive the climactic transformation. He may turn barbarous, atavistic, and idle. He may forget the sciences and arts that he invented, just as the Arab lost his mastery of mathematics and astronomy.

Or he may choose not to. After proving his capabilities in excavating the Equilateral, man will be ready to learn from

Mars how to assemble the social, spiritual, and material resources necessary to survive a dehydrating planet. Mars may
well be the force that makes us truly civilized, truly kind to
each other, wise, prudent, responsible to the natural world,
courageous in facing our global challenges, and, paradoxically,
truly human. Contact and communication with Mars must be
the next step in human evolution. This is what Thayer believes
and what he has told his audiences.

THIRTEEN

The heat demands that they travel after the sun goes down. Two lines of camels transport the swaying, muttering fellahin. He rides among them, dozing in his Bedouin saddle. Every so often the beast's missteps jolt him awake, and Thayer is momentarily surprised to find himself there, the animal beneath him skeletal, sinewy, and hideous. The dead country is hideous too. No token of intelligence lies within his sight . . .

. . . Until he lifts his head. The Milky Way spills across the sky in a riot of light, its component stars rampaging from Sagittarius to Cassiopeia. Thayer wishes that he was already returned to Point A, where he can open the observatory. The plodding steps of his dromedary reminds the astronomer that on his own planet man lives as solitary as an anchorite on a wave-battered rock. His only companions are the animals over which he holds dominion: he can ride them, he can harness them, he can pet them, he can expect loyalty from some, and he can eat and skin them. But he can't converse with them, not profitably.

Yet each of these stars may illuminate a world on which dwell creatures no less conscious than man; they may enjoy an intelligence and an appreciation of existence more advanced than our own, perhaps far more advanced. Their worlds may have been in contact since men lived in caves. The sky may be congested with intellects and as lively and swarming and raucous as the Soho Bazaar on the Saturday before Christmas. We can't hear their voices, but at this very moment sophisticated minds call to each other across the tangled, overgrown sky: instructing, inspiring, debating, and sharing their joys and sorrows.

The dragoman murmurs, "I believe it has been written so. The Forty-second sura."

Thayer was unaware that he was speaking. He thought the translator riding alongside him was asleep. The man's a young Cairene, with a jet-black beard and a neatly pressed galabiya, yet his eyelids are heavy and creased, heightening the typical impression of shiftiness. As dragomen go, he's been competent enough, though Thayer can't trust him to render fully what he's said to the fellahin or what the fellahin have replied.

"The Prophet," the dragoman says, taking note of Thayer's confusion. "The verse in the Quran: 'And one of His signs is the creation of the heavens and the Earth and what He has spread forth in both of them of living beings.'"

"I doubt that applies," Thayer snaps. "Mohammed was an illiterate trader nine hundred years before Copernicus. He couldn't have been aware of life on other planets."

When the dragoman bows, his head vanishes behind the hood of his cloak. "I'm certain you're correct, Effendi. What I know of the Quran and what the Quran may yet reveal are to each other only as a fragment of a grain of sand compares to a desert far greater than the one we traverse tonight."

They ride for a while and Thayer, irritated, observes that the dragoman's asleep again, if he was ever awake. In the moment before the Arab interrupted his thoughts, Thayer almost heard the celestial intercourse above his head—if not the actual words, then its beat and hum, its susurrations and sibilations.

On his own planet the man of intelligence is the loneliest creature of all. Thayer rides in a caravan of the illiterate and the ignorant, the faithless and the fanatical, for whom the waking state and the unconscious hold no important distinction, across a wasteland in which nine hundred thousand similarly shallow souls, dispersed in their rugs and buried in their trenches, drowse while their mouths work soundlessly in their slumbers, their muscles twitch, and their dreams remain incoherent.

He raises his head again and his eyes fill with starlight.

FOURTEEN

A pit about forty feet deep has been opened in the trench on Side AC at mile 191, near Sitra. A pyramid assembled from blocks of stone stands partially uncovered within the hole, its apex only a few feet above the plane of the side's excavations.

Thayer walks with care along the circumference, the Greek foreman at his side. The pyramid's unweathered, neatly fitted stones are coolly luminous, nearly transparent. One of the cubes near the top has been removed, leaving a black space through which snakes a rope ladder.

The foreman says, "This is an important discovery, sir. No one has found anything like it so far west of the Nile. Other pyramids may be buried nearby."

The monument is an ideal form made real, hewn from the rough, amorphous, uncooperative, imperfect, inexact Earth. Thayer nods at the ladder.

"Your men have gone in?"

"Only to investigate. Nothing was disturbed."

"Did they reach the base? How deep is it?"

The foreman candidly grins. "They tied six ladders together

before they reached the bottom. Then we removed the ladders and measured the total length. I swear, we could not believe it. The pyramid's depth is four hundred feet!"

Thayer takes another walk around the structure. Each of the exposed faces appears to be equilateral.

The foreman whispers, "We found treasures, sir: golden bulls, rams of porphyry, papyrus scrolls on which are written the histories of unknown dynasties . . ."

Thayer does the calculations in his head, estimating that the surface area of the four triangular sides and the square base is about eight hundred thousand square feet. Let's say each block is four feet deep: then beneath his boots are more than three million cubic feet of stone, transported to this stoneless plain four thousand years ago. The stones, like those of the famous pyramids at Gizeh, would have had to be quarried in the Arabian mountains, transported down the Nile and across the desert, and then assembled to a height greater than St. Paul's Cathedral—without the use of pulleys or the convenience of wheels, or the luxury of a lever.

"But we did remove one artifact, sir. It's a kind of toy or device."

Thayer takes the machine. It's a simple drafting compass, perfectly preserved, two flat arms of beaten metal hinged at their ends, their other extremities terminating in still-sharp points. A straightedge must have lain beside it. With a straightedge, a man may score a line segment on stone. Taking up the compass, he may then draw two circles around the segment's end points, each circle the same diameter as the segment. The circles will intersect at two points; each of those points is the vertex of an equilateral triangle drawn from the segment's end points, according to the first proposition of Euclid's first book, composed in Alexandria. The man may then go on to draw lines of equal lengths and manipulate lines and quantities that are unequal. With a straightedge and a compass he may plot further triangles right, acute, and obtuse, and then larger polygons; he

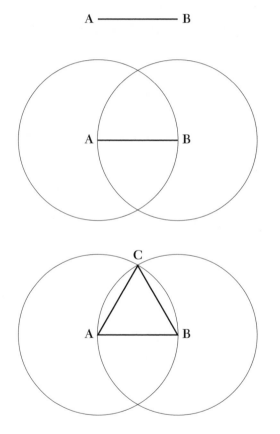

Euclid's first proposition.

may contemplate solid geometry. He may invent quadratic equations. He may survey the lands annually irrigated by the Nile. He may predict the motions of celestial objects. He may create a civilization.

The pyramid must have been seen as an impossible endeavor by the savants of its time, yet the builder had maintained confidence in its completion. He knew that his idea for the monument, whatever the enigma of its purpose, was as perfect as his geometry. If the pharaoh ran short of funds, if the slaves rebelled, if the Nile ran dry and grounded the fleet of barges that were tasked to bring the stones from their distant quarries, the geometry's integrity would restore the project, compelling flawed men to kneel at the altar of its flawlessness.

"Thank you, but there's no time to be lost," Thayer says. "Please bury it again so that we can lay the pitch. We have to finish excavating the segment. My friend, Mars will not wait."

FIFTEEN

Within days certain twittered, rumored threats fledge into actual trouble at mile 94 on Side BC, a segment of which is being paved by a squad of about two hundred men. The fellahin put down their spades and sit alongside them in the unremitting glare of the day, refusing to stir until their grievances are met. Two men are selected to present the demands, which are inchoate and unrealistic—more likely to be answered by Allah than by representatives of the Concession. The foreman has the delegates flogged in full view of the company. He empties the contents of the water cart into the sand.

News of the revolt spreads faster than the speed by which the fleetest runner can possibly communicate it to the other work sites. Strikes are called by companies on Side AC and at mile 180 on Side BC. Scuffles among workers break out farther down the side, too distant to be seen by their colleagues, who seem to know of them anyway. Thayer doesn't learn of the strikes until he's summoned by Ballard. The engineer has just returned from the pitch factory, where he was investigating the latest production delays.

Thayer hurries to Ballard's offices. The engineer is already in conference with the commander of the Nubians, accompanied by the segment managers in camp, most of them Europeans or Greeks and Turks. Thayer was probably notified as an afterthought, and not for his expertise in dealing with insurrectionists. Ballard wants only to remind him of what the project is up against.

The Nubian detachment is hardly adequate, with too few men and too few guns. When the Khedive, distrusting a new foreign military presence beyond those guarding the Canal and his ports, insisted on a small national guard for the project, the Powers chose not to contest the point. They had won agreement in favor of the Concession on nearly every other issue. The Nubians' only strength is their contempt for the fellahin, who in turn hate them for their khakis and their marginally higher pay.

The soldiers' captain, a florid Welshman, served Her Majesty in India for three decades, but Thayer knows Ballard finds him dodgy. The man listens to the report of the strike without asking questions or acknowledging the rebellion's severity. When the meeting disbands, several of the engineers exchange grimaces of concern. The Nubians ride off into the desert, kicking up plumes of sand before they vanish.

△

That evening rumors dire and persuasive ripple through the European quarters. The whites extinguish their lamps and turn in early. They hear the following: foremen have been killed; Point B has been overrun; the fellahin have joined with Mahdist dervishes and are marching on Point A. Although a detachment patrols Point A's perimeter, the Europeans are reminded that without the consolations of civilization, specifically loyal rifles, they're essentially alone in an indifferent desert. Dervishes were seeded among the fellahin months earlier. The whites listen for unusual sounds, yet the desert's every sound is unusual, manufactured by small animals beyond their acquaintance.

Given these circumstances, ordinary gallantry minimally demands that Thayer offer the secretary his company as night falls. He says, "Dee, I believe we have a game of chess left unfinished."

"Your total annihilation is what's left unfinished. I'll put up the tea."

They have plenty to discuss over tea, especially the shortfall in pitch production, which has been delayed at the satellite factories located throughout the Equilateral. Point B's plant is hardly operating at all. The entire enterprise seems to be slowing down. Miss Keaton has seen reports of prodigal water consumption. Excavators at mile 165 of Side AB have encountered previously unmapped marshes. In Europe an influential German philosopher has spoken out against an exchange of ideas and technology with Mars, speculating that its inhabitants will be so far advanced that they will make irrelevant our every endeavor in the sciences, industry, the arts, and ethics—circumventing millennia of future accomplishment and history. Man's inquisitiveness will be extinguished; his character will be degraded. Some newspapers have taken up the argument.

Thayer and Miss Keaton occupy plush upholstered armchairs, facing each other across a tea table. Floor rugs and a walnut armoire furnish the tent much like Thayer's Cambridge study.

As in Cambridge, the walls are emblazoned with maps of Mars, Egypt, and the night sky.

Yet the astronomer and his secretary exhaust their conversation once the reports have been discussed. They're aware again of the quiet beyond the tent, where the regular hum of Point A's thousands has been stilled. Thayer and Miss Keaton may well have been abandoned. They have yet to address their chess pieces, which remain where they left them weeks ago, ranged across the board, each fixed within the plane of its allowable motion.

Thayer says at last, "I don't think there are any dervishes."

"No, probably not."

"Ballard believes in them," Thayer observes.

"He needs to. He thinks they must lurk there beyond the glare of our fires, beyond our mortal ken, watching us—either for good or for ill."

"For ill, he's confirmed it."

Miss Keaton says, "That's because he's never built anything without opposition from the native population. He believes he's excavating against the forces of backwardness, paganism, and unreason as much as he's countering . . ."

"The weight of loosely packed sand."

"Exactly," Miss Keaton says, followed by a brief, arid laugh.

The gaslight has infused itself into her hair, incandescing the dried, inflexible filaments. Miss Keaton's eyes seem to be lit as well, though this must be an illusion, for the lamp stands behind her. The pleasure Thayer took in completing her thought lasts for only a moment, for then he recalls grievous instances of backwardness, paganism, and unreason from each end of the Equilateral to the other two.

"Yes, it's always difficult to make the locals comprehend what you've come for," he murmurs. Unsettled by the rebellion, wearied, and perhaps overcome by his familiar weaknesses, he permits himself another long look at her. She's surrounded by a nimbus of gold, like the icons in the Coptic monastery a few miles from the triangle's northern apex. "Dee," he says lazily, "don't you remember the porters in the Atacama? They were resolute in their noncomprehension."

Thayer realizes at once that he's trespassed. She freezes. The Chilean porters: they were red Indians and half-breeds, either impassive or sullen, draped in gaudy wool ponchos. They were convinced the visitors were prospectors, in a region well known to be worthless in minerals. They would bring Thayer rock samples every few hours, claiming they were of surpassing value. Once Thayer erected his telescope in the direction of the heavens, they refused to look through it, knowing there were no rocks there. Thayer and Miss Keaton have not spoken of the porters before, nor of anything that happened during the weeks of the expedition, save for its most important result: the paper in *Astronomische Nachrichten*, confirming that star formation can be witnessed in the Southern Hemisphere nebulae. Now he damns himself for his tactlessness.

She tentatively relaxes her expression. She looks at him carefully, wondering for what purpose he has directed her thoughts back to Chile. The time of night has affected her too. She says, "Chile." The beginning of a smile is raised at the vertices of her mouth.

But now something's changed in the night air. A new sound, muffled and slithering, has been introduced. For a moment

Thayer and Miss Keaton have been keenly, almost predatorily, aware of each other; now their vigilance turns outward. Miss Keaton's smile deliquesces. Before their alarm can resolve itself, a rustle at the entrance turns into a form and the form becomes real, small, girlish, and familiar. It's Bint, who may come at all hours of the day and night but usually makes her presence known only in stages.

She's visibly frightened. The rumors have reached the dormitory somewhat heightened, accompanied by stories of abduction and rape. The whites assume that they themselves are the targets of the insurrection, but in a lawless place a female of whatever race or nation is just as vulnerable as her Christian sisters. Bint sees safety here. She stands in expectation, her eyes wide, begging to be protected.

For want of anything to say in a language that she may comprehend, Thayer motions that she should pour the tea.

They're relieved. A question was posed, but it no longer has to be answered. Thayer realizes that his heart is pumping unusually fast, as if the fever has returned. The heart will slow. The heat that coursed through him was probably the fever all along. Miss Keaton removes one of his pawns from the board.

They expect that Bint will now disappear into the shadows, but she remains at the side of the table, waiting to pour another cup of tea. She's afraid to leave. She shows no surprise that Thayer and Miss Keaton are alone in Thayer's quarters so late. She wouldn't be able to imagine what the Europeans do when she's not attending them. In any event, she may suppose that Miss Keaton is one of Thayer's wives.

Miss Keaton declares check and observes, after Thayer blocks her queen, that he's left his surviving bishop unprotected. She takes it and after a few further desultory maneuvers his king is trapped. The board's geometry is unforgiving.

Annoyed, she studies the man, who has become inattentive. He barely looks at his pieces. He fidgets. The girl's still here.

Outside there are more sounds, some of them inexplicable. Night has fallen completely, yet most of the camp's Europeans remain awake with their guns at their sides.

SIXTEEN

Thayer and Miss Keaton step from his tent when the troops arrive, the Nubians' horses snorting with pleasure at leaving the loose sand that still lies between the Points of the Equilateral. Eight ringleaders have been brought back, one for each troublesome company. For all the unease that they've engendered among the whites, the men are wretched creatures, ragged and bruised, exhausted and dehydrated. One prisoner's right temple is gashed crimson. He has to be carried from the litter.

A scaffold is being erected, a device of elegant simplicity: an elevated platform; two uprights supporting a horizontal beam braced by crosspieces; a pair of ropes; and a trapdoor cut into the platform. The door is attached to the platform by iron bolts, which will be released by application of a single lever located at the edge of the platform. It's a universal tool. Any person of any nation, at any time in human history, would understand the machine's operation.

Ballard joins them. Sensing disapproval in Thayer's clinical gaze, he says, "A mutiny in the desert is no less dangerous than aboard ship."

The astronomer responds mildly, "The men can be sent off."

"Without mounts, that would be crueler than a hanging. And we can't spare mounts."

Two workmen clamber over the rough, unpainted structure, stopping to hammer at exposed nail heads in the fresh yellow pine imported from the Levant. A carpenter tests the trapdoor. The hinges squeal above the murmurs of the assembling witnesses.

Thayer privately speculates what his colleagues on Mars will make of this appliance. Their anatomy may not include a vertebral structure connecting their heads to their bodies, but once they're appraised of the scaffold's operation and purpose, they'll likely find it barbaric.

His mind clouds at the prospect. The Equilateral was conceived to benefit the whole of humanity. It's meant to promote the global commonweal and prefigure the other great projects—waterworks, dams, the outlawing of war, industrialization, universal public education—that will eventually draw on the talents and energies of men regardless of nation. This is how, in the last decade, he has presented his vision to the world's leaders and bankers, as well as to prominent scientists, philosophers, and religious figures. This is how the enterprise was proposed to the readers of the Sunday newspaper supplements. This is how it's understood by the children who went from door to door and slid coins into their slotted "Mars tins." None of them anticipated the scaffold, whose shadow on the sands is as black as ink.

Thayer says, half to himself, "At a time when we're plagued by the shortage of labor, we're about to give up eight workers."

Ballard scowls at Thayer's unease. "We'll hang just two, in fact. The others will be spared, allowed to return to their spades invigorated by fear. And edified, having been introduced to the concept of Christian mercy."

"Fear . . ." Thayer mutters. "Is that our greatest motivating force? Is there no ideal, no greater purpose, that may appeal to the men?"

"Fear works surprisingly well. That's been my experience, from Aswan to the Punjab."

"But the fellahin may not share our dread of pain or death. How else can they live in such miserable conditions? What fear can spur them?"

The chief engineer says darkly, "The fear of being made more miserable. The Arab has no ambition save to prevent further inconvenience to himself. Hanging is a decided inconvenience. In any case, Thayer, the decision's out of your hands. I'm the one commissioned to dispose of hindrances to the excavations."

Miss Keaton, who has been involved in nearly every discussion of logistics since their first meeting with Sir Harry, has attended this exchange from a distance. Her face is soft and unfocused. Overnight, while Bint lurked in the shadows, Miss Keaton and Thayer dozed off in their armchairs. When she woke she was confused about how she came to sleep there. For a moment—or for less than a moment, say for the time it would take for a beam of light to traverse the heavily worked line between Point A and Point B—she thought she was in Chile. Then she recalled there was a message that she was meant to receive from Thayer; also one that she wished to return.

Ballard presumes she's about to object, because her lips have just pursed and her eyes have opened wide, and also because ladies always object when they learn the stern measures that have to be taken to get something accomplished. The engineer credits Miss Keaton with a certain degree of competence, but he's still wary of her femininity.

He says quickly, to the astronomer, "We've already conceded that we won't be done by June the seventeenth. The Flare will be delayed. Most of the Equilateral may be excavated this summer, but I can assure you, Sanford, that for there to be any possibility of completing it at all, by any date, then stoppages and sabotage must be put down."

Thayer objects: "We haven't conceded June the seventeenth."

Ballard waves at his declaration. "For all intents and purposes—"

"It's six weeks away!"

Ballard welcomes the opportunity to speak bluntly. "None of the sides are more than three-quarters excavated, Thayer, and less than half the area has been surfaced. You've been out to the sites. You're aware of the obstacles. As for Side AB—you can see from here that we've made progress on the line segment radiating from the Vertex, but the excavations around mile one hundred haven't begun yet. Taking this into account, I'd say that the entire undertaking is hardly more than fifty percent complete."

"Fifty percent!" Thayer cries. Miss Keaton flinches, suddenly aware of the argument.

Thayer has known there were delays, but he never believed the Equilateral was this far behind schedule. "How can it be?

What have the men been doing for the last two years? We won't
be done for maximum elongation."

"As I've said, Sanford."

Thayer tries to collect himself. He turns his back from the
scaffold, past Miss Keaton, deliberately not looking at her. He
recalculates the problem: the current progress of the excavations, the number of men required, the amount of material
needed.

"So . . ." the astronomer begins, speaking into the vacant air.
"We have to increase pitch output. Let's have new manufacto-
ries built at the side midpoints. We'll assign fresh crews to Side
AB, at miles one hundred, one-twenty, and one-sixty; men
should be dispatched from Point B as well."

Ballard replies, "If only we had them. If only they'd work
like honest English navvies."

Thayer nods and gazes again into the plain as the new men
arrive at Point A from unmarked points, aspiring to apply their
muscle to the soft, liquid sands. But no, it's a desert mirage. The
Equilateral's being snatched from his grasp by thuggery, by il-
literacy, by superstition, and by indolence.

He levels a hard stare at Miss Keaton.

The secretary quickly responds: "There were problems while
you were ill. I've tried to keep you informed."

She has in fact been scrupulous in her accounting of the excavations. Nothing was withheld, though he was often insensible
when she read him the reports.

Ballard waits a moment, to let Thayer's anger ripen.

Then the engineer says, "The forces arrayed against us have
strengthened themselves, in the ranks of the fellahin and be-

yond. The mullah of Jerusalem has issued an edict against the Equilateral. It's *haraam*. Parliament's angry about the delays. They've threatened an investigation into the Concession's finances. That's why we're taking desperate measures."

"No, of course, I understand," Thayer says, his face gone pale. "But I won't give up June the seventeenth, not at any cost. When would we set off the Flare if not on the seventeenth, when it will mean the most and be most unambiguously observed? Do whatever is necessary."

The canal-builders, in the course of their history, must have also contended with brutes who would have scuttled their race's progress. The construction of the water transport system on which life on the Red Planet depends would have required fierce determination. It would not have been put off by bourgeois morality. Rebellions would have been subdued, perhaps with force. Vast wars would have roiled the globe's surface. They would have included the mechanized butchery that has accompanied our own military strife, augmented by more advanced and more gruesome weaponry. So Mars will not judge us harshly. The planet's history will show that conflict was ended only through the application of the universal laws of evolution and natural selection, when the superior and inferior specimens of the Martian race diverged into separate species, as is inevitable on Earth. A race of savants and a race of slaves, with breakable necks or not.

△

The fellahin are assembled. On this occasion no one speaks to them. The men know they've come for the hangings, and the reasons for the hangings are no more mysterious than their spades, the sun, or their thirst. The condemned stand above the crowd, at the edge of the platform, not looking at the fellahin, nor paying attention to each other. Perhaps they resent sharing the stage. In the minute before the nooses are drawn tight, their swarthy faces darken further. The lights in their eyes have already gone out when the empty sacks, which once contained flour, the wholesome odor of which occupies their nostrils, are lowered.

But something is wrong with the mechanism or the way one of the nooses has been tied or placed, and though the door drops cleanly, punctuated by a dramatic concussion when it hits the underside of the platform, the man on the right dangles alive from his rope for a full minute. His companion has obediently gone slack, his toes pointing to the ground, but the second man kicks his feet with force and precise direction, as if at a stubborn mule, while he suffocates. The carpenter-executioner looks on helplessly and turns to Thayer for guidance. Thayer can only glance away, embarrassed.

The fellahin don't object to the hangings and they've brought a certain holiday anticipation to the affair. The doomed man's struggle, however, commences a low-pitched humming within the audience. The murmurs spread among the fellahin and build as the prisoner audibly chokes. Thayer recognizes the hum as kin to the protesting drone that has accompanied the excavations from the insertion of the first spade. He hasn't identified it before. After making one last violent exertion, which twists his body as if he's trying to slip it through a closing doorway, the man finally expires. Justice has been done, but not without recalling the failures of equipment and personnel that have compromised the Equilateral so far.

△

The Earth is an elusive subject for the telescopes of Mars, showing phases just as Venus, Mercury, and the moon exhibit in ours. When the full daylit face of the Earth is visible, our planet always lies on the other side of the sun, a tiny object lost in the solar glare. As the Earth catches up with Mars, increasing its apparent size, our sphere shows the Red Planet more and more of its nighttime side. At maximum elongation, June the seventeenth, the portion of the Earth facing Mars will be half lit; only for a few of the following weeks, after the minutes in which the Flare blazed from Egypt's night shadows, will the daytime lands be sufficiently well placed to show their new equal-sided triangle. By October, when the two planets are closest, the surface of the Earth will not be visible to Mars at all.

Each civilization must wait its turn to view the other.

SEVENTEEN

No one conveys the order to have the gallows removed and it remains in place after the fellahin return to work. By chance the device has been installed in the single unobstructed location where it may be seen from anywhere in Point A, from the door to the hammam, from the pitch factory, from the mosque, from the windows of the commissary, from the dormitories, and from the observatory. Thayer finds it several hundred yards before him, at the end of a long allée of tents, the moment he exits his quarters.

The astronomer listens to the camp at work. Machines are being fired up and men perform their assigned labors, but this afternoon, several days after the hangings, their reverberations reach him subdued. They're accompanied by an undertone, the same distant strain of discontent that he recognized several days ago.

He wonders again how the inhabitants of Mars will read the Equilateral's difficult history. With their moral development so far advanced, the severe measures taken against the laborers may remind them of their own vanishingly remote, shamefully medieval past. They may judge man too savage to conceive of

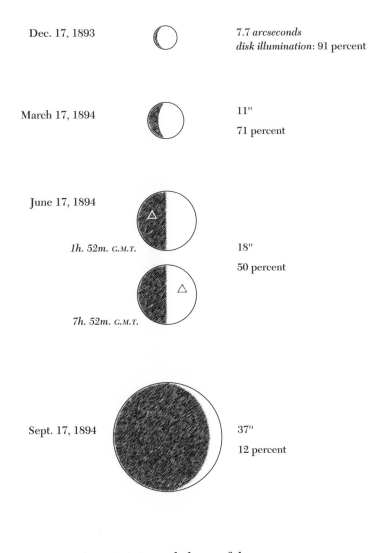

Dec. 17, 1893   7.7 *arcseconds*
disk illumination: 91 percent

March 17, 1894   11"
71 percent

June 17, 1894

1h. 52m. G.M.T.   18"
50 percent

7h. 52m. G.M.T.

Sept. 17, 1894   37"
12 percent

Apparent size and phases of the
Earth as seen from Mars, 1894.

friendship with him, nor imagine any sort of profitable exchange at all.

△

The sun's forced march toward its solstice point brings longer days and greater heat, shattering records that were set in the desert the first summer of operations. The fellahin demonstrate commensurately amplified lassitude. There are more cases of sunstroke, or at least claims of sunstroke, the excavators dropping their spades and falling to the ground theatrically. Thayer receives daily accounts from the work sites. Crews employing hundreds of fellahin seem to be immobilized at mile 105 on Side AB, digging out the same sand every day.

"What's wrong with them?" Thayer cries in frustration, dropping his fist on Ballard's latest report. "Do they want to remain at mile one hundred five? Do they believe they've found Paradise there?"

"Yes, the desert is strewn with figs and virgins." The engineer grimaces. "We offer the men instruction. We carefully translate. We account for differences in culture and national development. Still they refuse the lessons."

EIGHTEEN

Nearly every day brings news of another fatality. Today's death occurs inside the pitch manufactory: a scaffolding gives way. Six men are trapped in the debris. Besides the fatality, one of the men loses a foot, another an eye, and two claim internal injuries of an unspecified nature. Thayer wonders why there is still scaffolding within the building, which began operation nine months ago. He wonders too how a man can so easily lose a foot; specifically what did the man fall against or into that caused his foot to be severed? In the last two years the Arabs have proven to be as prone to injuries as a circle of elderly society matrons.

Thayer rides to the factory, a three-story brick structure close to the actual Vertex of Sides AB and AC, a confluence of uniformly paved pitch nearly as large as the Point A encampment itself. Inside the building the collapse has left an amount of debris that seems far greater than the mass of the scaffolding and whatever it supported could be. Workers pick through the rubble, choose items, examine them casually, and then return them to the piles. The foreman says it will be a week before the factory is again operational.

The astronomer says, "Make it three days and that'll be twenty pounds for you, placed directly in your account."

The foreman doesn't respond to the challenge.

Thayer climbs a still-intact staircase to the fourth floor, where there's an open porch. He steps out and sharply draws in his breath. For the first time from that elevation, he views the Equilateral's pitch-filled lines glistening wetly as they diverge from the Point A Vertex. They vanish toward points exactly sixty degrees apart on the level horizon. The foreman stands beside him, unseeing and indifferent, but Thayer is suddenly electrified, forgetting the haphazard labors going on beneath his feet. Here is the Equilateral made tangible. The pitch's blackness is stark against the luminosity of sand and sky, the Vertex pavement like a vast hole about to swallow the Earth itself.

When Thayer finally descends, he's inspired to return to his quarters on foot. He turns his back on the factory shambles and enters the ever-changing city invigorated. Flat stones have been laid down some of the pathways, forming rough streets and boulevards. Despite the standstill in the excavations, Point A seems to have increased in size and in the complexity of its layout, with new neighborhoods tucked into or adjacent to the original industrial sections, proliferating ad hoc alleys and plazas where they were not foreseen. Hovels and low gray tents sprawl into the distance, across the sands. There are men he doesn't know, Englishmen and Europeans, who are startled to encounter him on the paths, and who bow once they recover themselves. The distinctive music of the closing century resonates throughout the encampment: the steam engine's roar and the clash of heavy machine parts. A visitor can very well imagine that the Concession was established for no other purpose than the founding of Point A as a desert metropolis. Minutes after taking his pleasure in the Vertex, Thayer is stirred by the sight of the settlement that has been engendered by his vision, his advocacy, and his unceasing labors.

Yet he's aware that there's been further violence. This includes blatant acts of insurrection leveled directly at the Equilateral; as well as strife traveling circuitously from abstruse causes toward obscure ends. Men are slain with pickaxes, with spades, and with knives in close fighting. Perhaps the sun, now penetrating Thayer's helmet, has something to do with it. Meanwhile, quinine is in short supply at the infirmary and several more water tankers have gone missing. Bedouins are said to be responsible, or looters from the Sudan. Ballard has raised the prospect of water rationing, though consumption among the fellahin is already closely guarded.

In response to the growing disorder, the chief engineer has designated a mud-brick building on Point A's outskirts as a lockup, according to terms set by the Concession with the Egyptian government. Thayer believes that it's in another part of the city, but his uncertain footsteps lead him there anyway and, despite his growing fatigue in the heat, he stops to look in. Just inside the doorway, on a straight-backed chair absent a desk, he finds an Egyptian policeman, a Concession employee, smoking a long red-clay chibouk. Upon the astronomer's entrance, the man abruptly stands at attention, the burning pipe still in his hands. His tunic is unbuttoned. Thayer announces that he wants to view the prisoners. For a moment the policeman remains confused and then, alarmed, he leads him to the back of the jail.

Thayer expects the criminals to be languishing in cells. In fact they're unbound and unmonitored, out-of-doors behind the building in an open lot that attenuates into scrub. The policeman blows a whistle and they assemble in a single sullen row, about a dozen of them with their arms at their sides, as prescribed.

The men are distinctly Arab—more Arab-looking, it seems to Thayer, than his more reliable excavators: blacker faces, beakier noses, more profoundly mournful eyes. Yes: he finds a profound mournfulness in their eyes, reflecting the tragic fatalism intrinsic to their faith and culture. He walks along the line. The fellahin avert their eyes, or focus them at a point in the impossible distance. He inspects their filthy shirts and long, loose trousers.

He stops at one of the prisoners, among the most disheveled of them. A mean scar runs above his right eyebrow. The fellah looks past the astronomer, ignoring him. Thayer addresses the policeman.

"Why is this man being held?"

"He's a very low sort, Effendi."

"I can see that, but what's his offense? Why isn't he at the excavations? We're feeding him and giving him water, yet the man lies about the yard day and night."

"The Guards brought him. I don't know the particulars. He was refusing to work, I believe."

Thayer stares directly into the man's face. "Do you speak English?"

The policeman says, "Effendi, he's from a small village. He hasn't been taught a thing in his life."

"Translate, then. Ask him why he doesn't work. Why isn't he being cooperative?"

The policeman speaks a few words. The fellah answers by flicking his head, a gesture that Thayer understands to be equivalent to a shrug.

"I'm sorry, he doesn't care to respond. He's sick in the brain, I think."

"Doesn't he care whether the Equilateral is completed?"

The policeman smiles with visible effort. "He doesn't understand the Equilateral, Effendi. I'm an officer of the police, but even for myself the Equilateral is a strange endeavor. We hear rumors about its real purpose. Some say you wish to speak to the stars."

"I do!" Thayer declares. "That's exactly it! Ask him if he would like to join me."

The policeman blinks as he considers the astronomer's admission. It takes several moments before he can put this in words the fellah can understand. This time there's no response at all.

"We may have chosen for our interview the worst of a bad lot," the policeman observes, anxious about the intensity with which Thayer is gazing at the prisoner. The other fellahin fidget and glare. They don't like standing in the sun, and they don't like being questioned. Thayer evidently doesn't realize that he and the policeman are the only figures of authority here, and that they're both unarmed.

Only inches from the prisoner's face, Thayer demands, "Do you have no manly ambition at all? Do you want to remain immured in squalor forever? Why do you waste this opportunity to bring a measure of grandeur into your life?"

The policeman struggles to understand the questions and compose their judicious translation.

Perhaps he doesn't fully or correctly accomplish this task, but the prisoner's attention is seized. His eyes catch fire. His reply to the policeman begins calmly and then runs off the rails. He becomes passionate. He vigorously jabs his finger in Thayer's direction. Even after he makes his point, he goes on. Several fellahin murmur in agreement.

"He's answered with an impertinence," the policeman explains.

"What did he say?"

"It doesn't matter, Effendi."

"What is it?"

The policeman frowns, troubled. He has never before addressed as high a personage as Thayer. He's aware that the astronomer's unexpected arrival may cost him his position. The prisoners may mutiny, and that may cost him his neck. He offers Thayer an apologetic shake of his head while he ponders the fellah's invective. The fellah has replied that his life is already filled with grandeur. He says the word of God lives within him and that God's word is sufficient magnificence for a mortal man. He quotes the Prophet: "Those are the ones upon whom are blessings from their Lord and mercy. And it is those who are the rightly guided." It's Thayer with his machines and his foolish works who lives in squalor, by which the fellah means squalor of the spirit.

Clearly the man is a Mahdist, but the policeman knows he speaks the truth. He again chooses his words carefully.

"He says that his corn wilts. His father's ill. His wife has borne a son, who has yet to receive his blessing."

Thayer doesn't reply at once. There's no shade in the yard. The heat of the day can't be distinguished from his recent fever. He recognizes that he hasn't received an accurate rendering of the fellah's speech. He doesn't blame the policeman. A regular translator, like one of the better dragomen, would enjoy a greater command of both languages and know which cultural concepts are held in common and which need to be bridged. Thayer believes everything may be understood in the end: an equal-sided triangle, the elaborations of trigonometry, the motions of celestial objects, the fundamental principles and aspirations of intelligence.

"Send him home, then," he murmurs. He adds fervently, "With my best wishes for the boy."

Thayer doesn't recall fainting, nor does he recall the prisoners carrying him to the chair in the policeman's office, nor the cup of tea being brought to him, nor Bint's arrival. She looms above him now, biting her lip as if he's a damaged item for sale at the bazaar. The policeman and the fellahin stand behind her.

She leads him from the lockup to his carriage, a springless, wide-wheeled *araba*, and takes the seat next to him.

"Thank you for coming," he says.

She doesn't respond.

They travel in silence for a while. He gazes from the carriage into the unfamiliar neighborhoods through which they must pass. Washing hangs to dry above the streets. Women bring back produce from the local markets. Children play in the ditches. It seems that every quarter is centered around a new mosque whose spacious courtyard is misted by the spray of a voluptuously flowing fountain.

Bint is looking away and it occurs to Thayer that she is somehow cross with him. This may have been expected. Any kind of dependence on an Arab engenders insolence, even if she's a simple, illiterate, probably much-handled serving girl.

He turns away too and sees a half-naked child gazing at the carriage in delighted surprise. Thayer throws him a coin.

Bint says, "This is no place for a casual stroll. You've been ill. If you die here, the project fails. We will never speak with Mars. We will never learn from them."

"Pardon?"

Her eyes flash.

"And when you put men to death, you place the Equilateral in moral jeopardy! It no longer serves the people. It serves . . ." She pauses before she decides on the next words. "The Devil!"

Still pleased by his encounter with the boy, who caught the copper in midair, Thayer almost grins at Bint's attempt at speech, none of which he can follow.

"I believed once that the Equilateral was the gift of God, directly from the mind of God," she says hesitantly. Her eyes are moist. She moans softly before she continues: "I believe that no longer. It is the work of man, with all the compromises and imperfections of man. But I have confidence that the Equilateral can still be completed. It may yet find favor in God's eyes, if we complete it according to His law."

Thayer is puzzled by the Arab girl's attempt at complex expression, which comes out as a series of freakish grunts and cries. He says, "I don't understand you at all."

Attentive to the muffled impact of the horse's hooves on the sand-blanketed pavement, Thayer wonders when they'll reach his quarters. They've been traveling through the settlement for what now seems like hours. He's lost sight of the pitch factory and other distinctive tall structures. The carriage rattles down crooked alleyways that spill out onto broad, dusty thoroughfares before the vehicle returns to another warren of small lanes and cul-de-sacs that is perhaps the same neighborhood as the one they just left. Bint has assumed a poutish scowl as she stares directly ahead, past the driver. Thayer reflects how tiresome these girls can be. He'll have her replaced this very afternoon.

The scent of jasmine reaches him. He can't imagine that an ordinary Arab serving girl would perfume herself, so either this is a natural scent, a compound analogous to the floral fragrance and exuded by her pores, or in fact an ordinary Arab serving girl does perfume herself, proffering another mystery of the East, one of the many arrayed about her: Bint's provenance, her desires and ambitions, what she's seen, and the arts in which she's been instructed, especially the carnal ones. He can't be surprised by the feminine affectation now, he's always sensed in the girl the heat, the light, and the natural passions that have necessarily been made recessive in European women. Even as he feels himself relapsing into illness, Thayer speculates about what may lie beneath her robe, the distinct tawny-dusky colorations of her naked self. He begins to regard her pout as nearly coquettish.

△

By the time they reach his quarters, where Miss Keaton waits anxiously, the day's heat has abated, but Thayer is running a fever. Bint and the driver remove him from the carriage. Coming from his tent, Miss Keaton observes the flush that mottles his face, his frailty, and also the tenderness with which he allows himself to be supported by the girl, and how it's reciprocated. He mumbles a vague good-afternoon to his secretary. The girl firmly propels him inside. Miss Keaton stands by the tent flap for a moment before realizing that the driver stands with her, patiently anticipating his baksheesh.

Bint sponges off the astronomer and later, when he wakes in the evening dusk, the events of the afternoon have receded down a dimly lit passageway. His determination to dismiss her flickers in and out of visibility.

NINETEEN

The Arab needs to be beaten. He demands to be flogged. He hungers for the cudgel and the whip, and a kick or a slap from his betters. He considers every blow a sign of respect, or even love, evidence that he has been judged worthy of discipline and instruction. Strike, strike, strike—and pray to wake him from his millennia-long torpor.

Yet except in difficult cases Ballard has forbidden the bastinado, the Spanish-imported flogging that breaks the small bones and tendons of a man's feet and often leaves him crippled for life. A cripple incurs dishonor. He begs at the mosque and the market, sprawled in the dirt to be sniffed at by dogs. He can't marry—but he can't excavate more sand either. Depending on circumstance, exquisitely balancing Christian leniency against the demands of their undertaking, Ballard has formulated other means of compulsion. The Arabs appreciate this, he says.

Miss Keaton notes that most of the fellahin bear with perverse pride distinctive marks or raised calluses on their foreheads that have emerged over a lifetime of bowing and scraping against their prayer mats. The prayer bumps usually assume irregular shapes, but she occasionally encounters a man with a knob so perfectly round and evenly raised from his head that she has to resist the urge to pull on its stalk. She has discovered bumps that are circular disks and bumps that form ovals for which the two foci can be computed. Some prayer bumps are small, some are grand dominating features that take up most of the region between eyebrows and scalp. Often these calluses bleed, scab, and fall off, leaving peculiar depressions on the foreheads, difficult to distinguish from the effects of cancer or venereal disease. She once met a man, employed in a warehouse at Point B where the spades are kept, whose forehead accurately mapped Trivium Charontis, the intriguing oasis slightly north of the Martian equator.

These prayer bumps are acquired characteristics, to be sure, not in the blood, not heritable. Yet nearly every Egyptian boy is destined to bow and scrape and be so disfigured. Every race of man is defined by qualities incurred through experience as well as attributes transmitted at birth; its virtues and faults are mutable across the centuries. A productive race's industry and respect for legitimate authority can be engendered no less than its good dentition.

Now she contemplates the canal builders of Mars, who have already dug broad waterways thousands of miles long and are extending them at great dispatch, under Earth's straining, watchful, ever-astonished eye. They've invented ingenious, powerful machinery for the task. They've given their machines noble purpose. They've comprehended their world's tenuous atmosphere, dwindling bodies of water, hardy flora, exotic fauna, and embattled intelligence as interrelated elements of a single imperiled environment. Mars evidently commands much better laborers as well: more disciplined than their terrestrial analogues, more committed to their planet's survival.

Yet the engineers of Mars and their laborers are no more than victors in a brutal rivalry to survive their environment, just as the men of Earth are. Competition is intrinsic to the character of every living thing, including the canal builders. To ensure their continued procreation, they may have developed through natural selection broad lungs with which to suck in their atmosphere's thin gruel. They may have gained long flexible appendages to transport themselves in low gravity more conveniently. The inexorable drive for survival must have demanded beings endowed with godlike capabilities and judgment. And through natural selection and nonbiological processes, through brutality and education, through calculated humiliations and measures of grace, by pitting every individual against the other to determine who was more suited to their purposes, the engineers would have forged a separate, servile race that has put its servility to productive use, for the salvation of the planet they share with their masters. That's what it's taken to carve their lines into the fourth planet's hard red rock.

△

Miss Keaton finds Thayer with Ballard in the central bureau, standing over the long drafting table on which maps of the Western Desert are laid out. When she comes in the men look up without seeing her. They're entombed in grim thoughts.

"Now we're making no progress at all," Miss Keaton announces. She's already seen the day's reports. "More delays, more breakdowns, more sabotage. We haven't excavated ten miles in the last week."

"The fellahin are useless," Thayer replies.

Ballard adds, "We should have hanged all eight."

"Twice," Miss Keaton says. "That would have done it, I'm sure."

The engineer glares; Thayer remains contemplative. The bureau is not as busy as it should be: a few clerks chat idly among themselves near the filing cabinets, while most of the desks remain unoccupied. The Turk from the water bureau studies some tanker requisition documents. He looks up at Miss Keaton. She turns away and recovers her purpose.

"Sanford. Mr. Ballard," she says. "I've given this some thought. We need better men to accomplish the task—stronger men, more dependable men. These are not the men of Egypt."

"The men of Egypt are entirely contemptible. Worse than Hindus."

"In that case, Mr. Ballard, we must forge new men—from the dross we've been given."

He shakes his head.

"From our first day here, Miss Keaton, we've sought to improve the workers—in health and in spirit. We've built them schools and mosques. The Egyptians have never had overseers as generous as we are. We've worked ourselves to distraction trying to summon from them their greatest strengths and virtues."

"I believe that may have been our error," she says. "To excavate the Equilateral, we can't appeal to the men's best qualities. We must appeal to their worst! To see our work completed, we have to employ the most refractory of the fellahin, the most rapacious, envious, dishonest, distrustful, and depraved of them."

Ballard mutters darkly, "They're worse than that. You don't know their depravity by half."

Thayer nods in affirmation. Depravity—yes, that's exactly what it is, these slowdowns and these strikes, this obstinacy, this refusal to cooperate in human history's grandest undertaking, its most elevating common enterprise. Depravity. The word strikes Thayer somewhere deep.

Miss Keaton says, "So we have to bring into play another fundamental force in human life: competitiveness, instilled into man by his species' fight for survival. Every individual, even the lowliest Arab, needs to come out ahead of his neighbor. The desire to win is universal, regardless of the stakes or the level of racial development." She pauses, to see if they're accepting her assertion. The engineer's frown has developed into a full glower. She says, "I propose a contest—"

"Ridiculous."

"Conducted among the work teams assigned to each side. Each worker on the first completed side will receive an extra week's wages."

"A week's wages," Ballard repeats. "That should bankrupt the Concession right away."

"The Concession's full value depends on the Flare being ignited at maximum elongation. And it's entirely worthless if we don't complete the Equilateral at all."

"We can't do it. We don't have the funds. There's already an inquiry into disbursements. The French have threatened to withdraw."

Thayer interrupts them, for the first time, to scoff: "And leave the triumph to Albion? I doubt it. The money can be found. It will be."

Shaking his head, Ballard realizes that the lady has reached her man. He has seen this happen time and again, a woman interfering: in the Nyasaland mines, on the Twante Canal between the Irrawaddy and Rangoon, and once more when they raised the Jubilee Bridge in Bengal. He says, "A day's supplemental pay is sufficient."

"I'll cable Sir Harry myself," Thayer declares. "I'll urge a full week of extra pay, and money placed in reserve for another competition, to complete the second side. It will take two weeks to get the amount authorized, but we have to announce the competition today, at this hour. I take full responsibility for the decision."

"You better. The governors will raise hell."

Thayer knows that at this late date Sir Harry will give in. The project has cost far more than originally envisioned, but in London, Paris, and Berlin the Concession's bankers have succeeded in performing whatever financial machinations have been necessary. The extra wages are in fact a trivial addition to this month's expenses, less than what it takes to bring them the water that keeps the men alive.

△

Thayer himself announces the competition from the most prominent structure in the center of Point A, the scaffold. A dragoman translates for the few hundred fellahin who are assembled there. It's a difficult assignment, for the astronomer employs abstract terms and sophisticated language. He's trying to tell them more than the terms of the contest. He's explaining, again, the fame that will be theirs once the Equilateral is realized. The dragoman struggles to keep up. For the fellahin Thayer remains a mysterious figure—another European, in a vest and tailored trousers, who spends most of his days alone in his quarters. Some understand him as the shaman who secretly directs their divine labors. In some hearts he inspires fear; in others loyalty and wonder.

Every fellah in attendance will be deputized to transmit to another company in the field Thayer's speech and the underlying rationale for the contest. Given the peculiar ideas embedded within his rhetoric—for example, about how competition allows a man to find his place in the social order, as if God were unable to locate it for him—the speech will be misheard and distorted, bent to the cultural and religious mores of its audience. The emissaries with the farthest to ride will have the most opportunities to adjust what they identify as the statement's inconsistencies, tautologies, and false antecedents. By the time the message reaches the farthest segments of the Equilateral, it will bear no relationship to what was said by the man who issued it, except of course for the promise of more pay.

△

After he's been lowered into his camp bed—the fever has returned—but before he can sink into oblivion, Thayer considers the transcript of his speech that will be composed by the Concession and at some time in the future made available to historians on our sister planet. They too may not understand the moral reasoning behind the contest. The premise of Miss Keaton's argument is that competition is ingrained in man's universal character because it's encoded in creation through natural selection, the most fundamental of all competitions. We don't know, however, whether Darwinian evolution is in fact a universal principle in every region of space. The development of Martian life may very well be governed by some other natural process that does not rely on mutation, adaptation, and natural selection.

If evolution is *not* a universal process, if competition is not a universal principle, if Mars is not subject to Darwinism, the planet's economy may have developed according to entirely different natural laws. How does Mars apportion its commodities and goods? What is the role of capital? Of labor? How is personal status attained? By what means are social hierarchies erected? Does Mars enjoy a gentler sex that raises its young and performs the traditional female duties? If not, then . . . Lying in his camp bed, his eyes closed, Thayer struggles to imagine how the inhabitants of Mars conduct their lives on their shrunken, withered sphere.

TWENTY

Whether because the fellahin understand the terms of the competition or because they've been frightened by the scaffold, which remains in place, work on the Equilateral assumes new urgency. Encouraging reports from the desert begin to arrive at Point A. With an influx of fresh diggers from Tripolitania, the excavation of Side AB between miles 100 and 220 is finally under way. The Libyans bring their own vocal compositions and vigor to the task. Before the first spade strikes, their imam blesses each segment to which they've been assigned. The pitch factories augment their output. Thayer asserts again that the Equilateral will be completed in time for maximum elongation. Mars is doing its part, moving into its best position to observe the Flare on the morning of June the seventeenth.

Thayer perceives that the mood in Point A has lifted. The men's shouts and oaths are less rich in complaint, more relevant to their duties. The fellahin don't look us in the eye, but their minds are now engaged to the needs of the Equilateral. The odor of fresh flatbread wafts pleasantly through the administrative quarters most mornings. Thayer has not established the location of the oven, but he presumes it's close.

They should have done this years ago, put their faith in competition: the strongest over the weakest, the industrious over the indolent. These are the terms that allow for civilized society's ascendance on Earth in the first place. Once more the universal laws have been confirmed.

But the winners of the competition have already been determined. Side AC was closest to completion when the contest was announced, and now nearly all its segments have been excavated. The Point C pitch factory has been steadily supplying the paving crews up and down the side. The petroleum piping is in place, with most of the problematic joints fitted. The fellahin aren't aware of this. They don't receive the reports and wouldn't be able to read them if they did.

△

The wall-sized map of the Equilateral in Thayer's tent now begins to show progress on each section. The astronomer can look at the map with satisfaction for twenty or thirty minutes at a time, just as he would gaze at a celestial body. Every notation on the chart announces a technical problem solved, a challenge met: another conquest for mankind.

Yet Mars may not be impressed by the Equilateral. Each visible segment of the red planet's canal system surpasses, by itself, the extent of man's global excavations. The astronomers and engineers of Mars will observe the Equilateral with amused, condescendingly benevolent smiles, if they have smiling-capable organs. They will find the greatest expression of our intellect and labor hardly less primitive than the ceremonial mask carved out by a Hottentot.

Or they will not understand man at all. Their minds may well be too distant from ours; too advanced or too different or too-something in a way that we can't comprehend. The astronomers of Mars will be aware that Earth has lit a massive fire on its surface precisely at the moment when the planet's position in the Martian sky is farthest from the sun. They will peer down at the Equilateral and observe its geometric perfection. But they may not find these phenomena sufficiently remarkable to record in their notebooks.

TWENTY-ONE

The courier from London delivers a week-old issue of the *Times*, and in the paper's illustrated section a long article by the Cairo correspondent confirms the Equilateral's progress. Based on an interview conducted by telegraph, he seconds Thayer's assertion that it will be done on schedule. Although flawed by several risible inaccuracies, the article properly reiterates what interplanetary communication promises for the ordinary man: the wisdom of an ancient race, its inventions and technologies, the opening of a vast new market.

Articles like this one have become familiar in newspaper supplements for a decade, as have sketches of the Equilateral, whose base now stretches eight columns across the page and is decorated with dunes, camels, and fanciful palm trees. (Not a single palm has yet been encountered on the plain.) At the top of the figure, like corks, bob four cameos of "Sandy" Thayer, Sir Harry, Ballard, and Miss Keaton, to her astonishment and embarrassment.

"This is uncalled-for," she cries.

Thayer is stooped over the newspaper, which has been laid

out on a drafting table. He doesn't immediately reply. After a while he looks up. "What's that?"

"My picture. I'm hardly a Concession panjandrum. I'm your personal secretary."

"That's all right," he says. He hasn't noticed the drawing. Now he studies it for a few solemn moments and raises his gaze to her. It's been a long while since her face was held in such steady regard, by him or by any man. His eyes return to the page. He pronounces, "It's a handsome likeness."

"I don't recall sitting for it. They must have spied on me aboard ship or when you addressed Parliament."

"Newspapermen," he declares. "The article is very foolish. They repeatedly say 'men from Mars,' even though I've told them time and again that, whoever built the canals and whoever observes the Equilateral, they're anything *but* men. They can't be, for they haven't evolved from the same organisms that men have." He reads on. "But I can't say I'm not pleased. Sir Harry will be pleased. This will be useful in raising support for Line CD."

Although Miss Keaton has long avoided the merest flutter of vanity, she can't help but be gratified by the sketch. It must have been done years ago, for the woman in the image is not the desert-dried spinster who encounters her in the mirror every morning. Miss Keaton glows now, against her will, for the caress of Thayer's close observation still lingers on her cheek.

This moment of female weakness leads to another, a few hours later, when the secretary looks up from her correspondence to watch as Bint pours water from a brown clay pitcher into a basin, one hand steadying the pitcher at its wide bottom. The girl performs this task with complete, cosmic stillness, like a statue that may have been unearthed from beneath the sands, yet she's as supple as a cat and as fecund as the Nile. Thayer burns for her, of course.

From long experience the secretary recognizes that Thayer's attentions regarding Bint are ephemeral and predictable, of no greater weight than those she's observed him direct, before they came to Egypt, toward other females. A shopgirl. A singer. Some kitchen girl, not unlike Bint, except that she was Irish: lithe, apple-cheeked, bright-eyed, with a giggle that carried throughout his drafty, many-winged manor in Cambridgeshire, where Miss Keaton shared his study. A parade of kitchen girls.

Thayer romances these creatures discreetly but without shame. He never speaks of them to Miss Keaton, even when it's clear that he's arrived from an assignation. Maintaining his accounts, she's aware of the gifts the girls receive, the pins, the hats, the necklaces, the wraps, and even the pair of Pekinese bestowed on an actress at the Gaiety. She senses that not a single affair has ended unhappily, with expectations unmet.

She wonders what trifle Thayer will find to purchase for Bint, out here in the Western Desert. She amuses herself with the thought before recognizing that it's the very irrelevance of pins and hats that lies at the core of his interest in the girl. He can never know what will please this strange, silent young woman from an anonymous Egyptian village, her mind sparking with references, assumptions, and personal histories that can't be fathomed, but he can study her and draw conclusions. This is what he likes to do. What he discovers will never be proven wrong, yet she will take the gift and may not even understand it's a gift.

Bint looks up and catches Miss Keaton's eye and the older woman smiles in candid admiration at her poise and elemental beauty. Bint's gaze in return is sharply alert; the alertness unsettles her. Miss Keaton feels something move in her face, a kind of tidal tugging. The secretary's smile fades, or becomes more complicated: part grimace, part frown, part grin. The new gesture is richer than she intends. It betrays her with a meaning, or a series of meanings, beyond admiration. They extend toward grief. She can't stifle it. The wounded smile expresses what she can't articulate to herself, yet in the girl's profound dark eyes Miss Keaton recognizes the warming glimmers of compassion. Perhaps even pity.

△

That evening, alone in his tent, Thayer reads the article more than once, and again he studies the small rendering of Miss Keaton, admiring the anonymous artist's talent. His touch is light but expressive, a rare balance of qualities for a newspaper illustrator. Thayer knows, as a principle of planetary astronomy, that the skilled hand may capture what lies beyond the eye's perceptive capacity: minute differences in shading, patterns and then meaning in apparently unrelated features, developments in progress, the past hidden beneath the static visage of the present, sometimes even the future. The artist may excavate from the observation of shifting, disparate, hardly glimpsable lineaments the most profound elements of beauty.

Dee had first come to his observatory in Kent in a hired trap, her expression direct, her eyes clear, with references that attested to her computational prowess. He had known her brother at Cambridge, a big-lunged sculler now a broker or lawyer in the City. When he met the young woman they did not speak of the brother, but only of objects millions of miles away, planets, stars, and nebulae. These were things they could know but never touch. She was prodigiously informed.

He puts down the *Times*. Under the lamp he observes that in the desert atmosphere the paper has already started to decay and its ink has begun to sublimate off the page, blurring the article's illustrations as well as the type. By morning the image will be gone completely.

TWENTY-TWO

The excavations' years of strife and disappointment are suddenly punctuated on May the sixteenth with news that Side AC has been completed, the pitch laid, and that the men, after receiving chits for their extra wages, will be dispatched to aid the crews on Sides AB and BC. Thayer knew that progress was being made, he saw the map being filled in every day, but the side's completion startles and delights him. The surprise derives not from lack of confidence in the Equilateral, for which he has had ample cause, than from doubt in the progress of time, so mired has he been in these unyielding sands. Just as he struggled in opposition to the fellahin's prejudices and the desert's austerities, so did he begin to imagine that time strains against the bulwarks of a static existence. But the final closing of the gaps in the side proves that time flows forward, inundating everything in its path. After the boy who brought the report departs, Thayer drums at his desk in satisfaction. He feels the need to embrace someone; the absence of someone to embrace produces a sudden ache in counterpoint to the joy that has flooded his being.

When Ballard comes by the next morning, the astronomer

KEN KALFUS

insists they ride out along the side. Flanked by a Nubian detachment, they set off in a caravan of camels and *arabas* on
the packed dirt track. The track runs parallel to the excavated
side, the level ridge where the removed sand has been banked,
and the main petroleum line, stretching from the southern horizon to an unseen place precisely thirty degrees east of due
north. Thayer is gratified by the care taken by the men in removing and packing the debris, which rises forty feet above
the track. About fifteen miles out, the caravan stops at a place
where their advance party has established a shaded observation
pavilion on the top of the ridge. The men have carved steps up
the steep slope and laid them with planks. In his excitement
Thayer bounds the first several steps two at a time, before realizing that he barely has the strength. One of the porters has to
take him by the arm, in a moment that Thayer will not recall.

There it is, the paved line beneath them, a great black oily
river. Between the two ridges of debris across the five miles'
width of the side, the line extends left and right. A string is
plucked in his heart. The Equilateral is real. It will be completed.
All Europe is watching—if not literally, then at least through the
dispatches of its correspondents, which even when they confuse
the astronomical and engineering details never slight the grandeur and nobility of the enterprise. Photographs have been
widely circulated. The consuls have cabled the reality of the
undertaking to their governments.

The neatly paved ditch reradiates the heat of the sun. Djinnis
and houris dance in the troubled air above it.

"The equilateral is the most visually satisfying, most inspir-

126

ing geometric figure of them all," Thayer says. "Did you know, Ballard, that the equilateral was the Hittite symbol of life? Pythagoras connected it to the Goddess of Wisdom. The Christians discovered the Trinity in it. You may see equilateral forms within the Doric portico and in the greatest edifices of the Church. The equal-sided triangle combines the virtues of uniformity with those of variety; it can be rotated three ways and look the same, and turned another three ways and still look the same; it's the component of all regular pyramidal solids, including of course the pyramids of antiquity; it demonstrates a completeness and harmony in itself. The equilateral is the basis for all human art and construction."

"Bloody difficult to dig, though."

Ballard draws on his cigar while Thayer looks into the trench, his eyes jolted by the contrast between the pitch and the embankment. A petroleum tap, connected to the main line by a spur buried under the ridge, gleams above the side's surface.

The chief engineer adds in a murmur, "And I don't know if it's the truly fundamental figure."

The climb has wearied Ballard perhaps more than it did Thayer. He smokes without pleasure, haggard.

"A case may be made for the primacy of the circle," the astronomer agrees. "While the equilateral is the basis for man's science and man's works, the circle is the only geometric shape that occurs in nature. Drop a pebble in a puddle and it radiates perfectly circular waves; certain microscopic cells are impeccably round; at the other end of the scale, so are stellar clusters like Omega Centauri."

For several minutes Ballard considers the paved side.

At last he says, "I wonder, Sanford. I wonder if we've excavated the wrong figure. The circle wouldn't do either."

"Pardon?"

"The equilateral triangle is an excellent thing, but I can think of an entirely different figure that is much more significant to most men. I speak of the cross. I appreciate that you favor basic geometric figures. I'm an engineer and I depend on them. But it's the cross that unites the world's civilizations. This is the symbol of our Savior's sacrifice, our God's love, the emblem of our faith. It's the cross, not the equilateral, that would have been the clearest expression of man's best nature to have been transmitted to Mars."

Although he's beginning to feel the effects of the day's heat, Thayer smiles benevolently.

"The cross may not mean to them what it does to us. They may not be aware of the Crucifixion. Did Christ die for their sins, or did the inhabitants of Mars extirpate sin from their racial character eons ago? I don't know. But I suspect that when a good Christian sits down with a Martian emissary, they will find they share the sentiments that we characterize as Christian: generosity, humility, and piety before the transcendent mysteries of the universe." Thayer adds modestly, "We can't rule out the notion that the traits we consider Christian today may be called Martian in the language of the twentieth century. Referring to your neighbor as a good Martian gentleman may prove the highest compliment."

"And what of this lot?"

Frowning, Ballard tips his head at the men who accompanied them to the site: porters, soldiers, drivers, diggers. They mill around the rampart, impatient to return to Point A. Some observe the paved side for the first time. Their hostility to it is barely disguised.

Ballard's anger overflows. "They need the cross! The cross! I want to excavate *a cross* in the desert—let it extend from Mecca to Medina! That would show the blackguards. Ignite the petroleum an hour before dawn on Easter Sunday. Bask in the glory of the Resurrection!"

Thayer observes Ballard's agitation. The engineer's eyes water and his face is flushed.

"I'm pleased you haven't lost your appetite for the excavations. AB and BC still need to be completed. But first let's go down to the pitch. I want to stand on the surface of the side."

△

Their dragoman objects: "Effendi, the temperature is more than a hundred degrees. The men are hungry and tired. If I may be permitted to make an observation, Professor, you appear fatigued as well."

But a stairway is cut into the ridge's other slope. As Thayer descends, the rising heat beckons to him like a newly discovered, life-giving star. When he reaches the pitch, just ahead of Ballard, he finds that the surface has baked hard and takes his weight without leaving a mark. The radiation burns through the soles of his boots. Acrid, tarry fumes swirl around him. Thayer stares at the sky, which is as solid as a piece of glass.

Even now Earth is emerging from the solar glare and Egypt's Western Desert lies within the eyepieces of distant telescopes.

Peering through their thin, changeable atmosphere, Thayer's colleagues on Mars wonder whether they're truly observing artificial features on the surface of the third planet. They make sketches and compare them to drawings composed months earlier, before the pale blue-green sphere went behind the sun. As Thayer takes a few tentative steps along the side of Triangle ABC, they dispute whether the regular lines they thought they observed last terrestrial autumn have been extended to form a regular geometric shape. Theories are advanced that these are natural features and the most eminent (and pompous) Martian astronomers have come forth to prove that they're the result of natural geologic or hydrologic processes. Other observers, with keener eyesight and more flexible intelligences, pursue their own happy hypotheses.

△

The dragoman's concern for the astronomer's durability in the heat proves justified. Ballard returns up the ridge and down to their carriage on his own steam, barely, but Thayer needs to be carried by the porters. He doesn't recall anything of the return to Point A. His only memory is a womanly cry at the end of it, as he's removed from the coach in blankets, shivering.

Now Bint feeds him broth. She speaks to Thayer often, in her own language, in reprimand, he thinks. He doesn't understand what she says, but he hears reproof—also worry, also sorrow. Sometimes she expects a response, as when she asks a question, to judge from her inflection, and then she waits, her eyes wide. Miss Keaton stands by, speechless with fright and impotence.

Throughout this new illness, or relapse—the doctors' diagnosis is ambiguous—Thayer keeps track of the days passing. Awareness of the day's date is the single fact he manages to keep in his head. He whispers it to himself when he sleeps and again when he wakes. If Side AC was completed on May the sixteenth, and it's a week since he fell ill, then, as the Earth remains visible progressively later and higher in Mars' western sky, they have hardly more than three weeks before maximum elongation.

TWENTY-THREE

int has made this journey before, slipping from Thayer's quarters while he sleeps. She's wrapped in a black shawl that has made her even more impervious to sight. She goes quickly from the administrative compound; taking an indirect path, since no direct path is available, she reaches one of Point A's residential quarters, where all the men are fellahin and the Equilateral is no more than a myth or rumor. She stops at the door of a certain crooked mud-brick house, in an alleyway of similarly modest homes. The door opens. Bint knows precisely what to ask for.

She returns from an entirely new direction, never once crossing her previous path. She's been gone for hours, but Thayer hasn't stirred in that time, and Miss Keaton did not look in. When the girl next makes tea, she adds something to the infusion, as she's done before, something colorless and tasteless and sustaining.

△

The doctors assemble. Thayer sleeps and they're gone and then Thayer sleeps and they've come back. Earth approaches maximum elongation; Thayer feels it in his blood. In one of the flickering interims of dark and light, he frames two whispered questions: "Side AB? Side BC?" The doctors don't respond or speak among themselves or to Miss Keaton. They have each privately confirmed that Thayer's affliction is not malaria; it is indeed Kharga Fever, which often results in loss of vision and sometimes a more complete state of blindness, namely death. Even when Thayer's fever breaks, contrary to the illness's usual course, they remain alarmed.

Yet Ballard arrives at the secretary's bureau one morning in elevated spirits.

"Progress, my dear Miss Keaton, progress!"

She's been looking at the reports. Once Side AC was completed, Ballard added teams to several segments on the rest of the triangle and has spurred the pitch factories into high production. Yet she distrusts the engineer's show of optimism.

"How do you mean?"

"Side BC's excavated and the last bit's being paved today and tomorrow. Side AB's coming along too."

"They finished Side BC? It's done?"

"But for the pitch."

"That's excellent news," she says warily.

"We may be completed before maximum elongation; it now seems possible." The engineer removes a sheet of foolscap from a stained, travel-beaten kit bag. "I need your opinion, Miss Keaton. What is this?" he says, holding up the paper to display a familiar geometric figure.

The bureau lamp flickers. Miss Keaton raises her guard. "It appears to be an equilateral triangle, but perhaps it's not."

Ballard insists, "It's bloody close."

"I don't think so."

"What's wrong with it? How is it not an equilateral?"

Miss Keaton rests her eyes. She sees a true equilateral cast against the pale black screen on the inside of her eyelids. The triangle's on fire.

When she opens her eyes, Ballard says, "I've already been in contact with London about this. The fellahin on Side BC were evidently overzealous in acquiring their extra wages. They went off the surveyed line. They veered northwest toward Side AC, with the connivance of their foremen. This happened about thirty miles from Point C. At the same time, I'm not sure how, they signaled their dodge to the corresponding workers on Side AC, who then turned sharply toward them. They eventually met at a point about eleven miles south of Point C. Call it C-prime, if you like. I'm told they've apparently established a tidy little settlement there."

"Damn them! This is sabotage!" she cries. "This is mutiny! The entire undertaking depends on the Equilateral's perfect form."

Miss Keaton doesn't know how much connivance there was between the chief engineer and the errant work crews. Perhaps this deceit was to be expected. Every engineer cuts corners. It may be intrinsic to the process of turning abstract ideas—infinite lines extending across boundless planes—into tangible, non-Platonic substance. Yet the Equilateral is like no other engineering project in the history of mankind: its tangible, physical reality *is* the Platonic.

She says, "It has to be rectified. They need to fill in the mis-

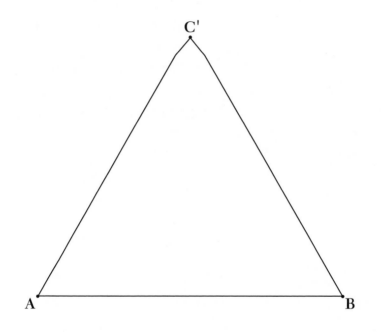

placed lines right away and excavate the new segments to Point C. There's no time to lose. Hire more fellahin."

"Miss Keaton, I'm afraid that's impossible. We're just a few weeks from maximum elongation."

"It *can* be done! For years men have been telling us that the Equilateral is impossible, that the funds could not be raised, that the fellahin could not be assembled and quartered, and that the spades, the water, and the petroleum could not be acquired and transported to the desert. They've been proven wrong on every count. The Equilateral can be completed and the Flare can be ignited—properly and in time!"

Ballard shows her the foolscap again.

"Look at this," he says. "It's a scale representation of a triflingly irregular polygon. The deviation from C to C-prime is a little more than four percent of a line drawn from C to the midpoint of AB. If you resketch it as an isosceles triangle, the angles at the base are just one-point-two-nine degrees less than an equilateral's. At their distance, the observers on Mars won't distinguish the figure from an equilateral triangle any better than you can."

"I can," Miss Keaton insists. "Anyway, it's dim in this room. I'm fatigued. You're not holding the sheet steady."

Ballard says, "Observers on Mars won't enjoy entirely favorable conditions either. Even at maximum elongation, they'll have to contend with the solar glare. They'll have to peer down through our wet, heavy atmosphere. And their telescopes' optical qualities will be limited, just as ours are."

"How can we be certain of that? We know nothing of their instruments. They may have telescopes capable of resolving

Point A itself. It's not impossible that they may observe the workers' quarters, the excavation equipment, the water carts—even the ruts in the sand left by the water carts!"

"If they're so far practiced in their telescopic skills, Miss Keaton, they won't have needed us to provide them with an equilateral triangle. Whatever their level of superiority, they'll forgive us our not-quite-equilateral. They'll recognize that we employ lazy, careless workers. They'll draw certain not-inaccurate conclusions about our civilization's immaturity. But they're scientists. They'll find our faults interesting, perhaps as lessons that give them perspective on their own distant, troubled past. Our shortcomings will be the subject of a report to the Mars Astronomical Society. Be at ease. We may yet make some Martian astronomer's career."

"Professor Thayer will be furious. *I'm* furious. While he's been ill, everything's been overturned—with only weeks to go. The poor man . . . This will break his heart."

"I think you're right," Ballard says evenly. "It's a blow. In his fragile condition . . ."

"You must reexcavate the sides!"

Ballard again shows her the figure. This time it startles her, bringing color to her cheeks.

"Sir Harry has seen this," he says. "He'll keep it to himself. We needn't tell the press. We needn't tell Professor Thayer. For the purposes of the endeavor, he's achieved what he set out to do. History will recognize him for that. We needn't let a trivial discrepancy spoil his moment of triumph."

"It's not trivial," she declares, but she concedes, through her rage, the insupportability of her position. A little more than 4 percent, 1.3 degrees. And if what's at stake is Thayer's well-being, even his life . . .

She shakes her head vehemently, looking away, down at her desk and the useless reports. She neither acknowledges Ballard's departure nor his suggestion.

TWENTY-FOUR

While the false Point C Vertex is excavated and lined with pitch—a blot in the desert, a stain on the endeavor, a rat that gnaws at Miss Keaton's shivering heart—the project nears completion and the Red Planet rises in the Egyptian sky, on its way toward opposition, just as Earth ascends in the violet, hour-long evening dusk of Mars. Further accidents are reported and additional work stoppages have to be curbed, and rumors of more insidious unrest percolates among the overseers, yet the Equilateral moves, like the silently gliding planets themselves, toward its appointment with maximum elongation. The last section of the petroleum line arrayed around the triangle is laid. Each of its three hundred and nine taps have been installed.

As anticipation of the Equilateral's completion seizes the fellahin, who continue to maintain an imperfect understanding of its purpose, Point A is jolted by news that the settlement will be inspected by the Khedive himself, said to be a monarch of cunning, culture, and enlightenment. He will be accompanied by no less a dignitary than Sir Harry.

The excitement's enough to rouse Thayer from his sickbed.

Bint gives him a haircut. He steps from the tent wan and un-steady, but he's fully heartened, not only by the coming visit, but also by the Red Planet's increasing proximity. Every day it's another half million miles closer to Earth.

Ballard is forced to take men off the Equilateral to pre-pare suitable accommodations and tidy up Point A, which after two years of hard service has fallen into a disorder barely remarked by its inhabitants. Latrines that have caved in have been incompletely filled. Chickens peck between tents, many of which are slack and roughly patched. A costly puddle of water leaks from the hammam. Broken machinery has been left where it failed. Unsightly structures have gone up adjacent to the Nag Hammadi track, in Point A's outlying districts and suburbs. Ballard orders them rebuilt. The engi-neer is furious at the delays entailed by these preparations, especially as the improvements will be abandoned in weeks, immediately after maximum elongation, when the project is concluded.

Thayer is surprised that Sir Harry himself is coming to Point A. The astronomer shared rostrums and headlines with him as the Concession's capital was raised, yet since ground was bro-ken he has become a reclusive figure, in communication with Thayer only intermittently, and usually only on the subject of expenses. This is his first journey to the Western Desert. It's unclear whether he still comprehends the project, and whether he still believes in it.

△

When the chairman of the Board of Governors is lifted from his carriage, the fellahin who are aware that he's a Knight of the British Empire wonder from which untimely, ill-favored Crusade he's returned. The pale and disheveled Englishman seems debilitated from the desert's rigors. The men set him on his feet. He takes a few steps forward and vomits onto the sands.

The astronomer announces, "Sir Harry, we welcome you to Point A, the Vertex of Angle BAC, the southernmost and westernmost point on the Equilateral! We hope to make your stay here as comfortable as possible."

Sir Harry replies, "It's certainly cost me enough."

The military orchestra assembles around the Khedive's carriage. The entire camp turns toward the vehicle. The royal fanfare begins and is aborted several times before the Khedive finally appears, his uniform neatly pressed, his cap perfectly set. A large man, with a barrel chest that bulges against his tunic, he waves as if vast armed legions stand behind the orchestra. He bows to Miss Keaton and clasps the hands of the astronomer and the engineer.

Due to the governor's indisposition, and also because of the intense heat, the welcoming pleasantries are curtailed to a brief rededication of the settlement, which is to be called Point Khedive Abbas Hilmi II in perpetuity. That evening a supper under the fixed stars and wandering planets is prepared by royal chefs with provisions brought from Cairo. Thayer delivers a stirring address that reminds his audience of the Equilateral's high purposes. Ballard reads the text written for Sir Harry, who is still ill and looks on balefully. The Khedive's remarks are reiterated in six languages. The company retires early, in preparation for the following morning's balloon ascent.

△

The machine has been shipped from London and inflated overnight in the scrub a few steps from the former site of the scaffold, whose remnants have been scrupulously removed. Beneath the swaying gas envelope an observation car is stamped with the words: MARS CONCESSION. The Khedive is delighted; he's said to take a keen interest in modern technology, examples of which, including telephones and flush toilets, are installed throughout his palace, according to amused visitors from the English colony. He briskly questions the pilot, a dark, taciturn junior officer in the Royal Navy who has served aboard the Khedive's Suez yacht, the *Mahroussa*. The Khedive poses a singularly original question. Did not Amenhotep III's Eighteenth Dynasty employ similar vehicles for flight? He recalls an inscription to that effect on the Third Pylon, in the Temple of Amun. The sailor replies in vague affirmation, assuring him that he's perfectly familiar with the balloon's classic Egyptian provenance, as well as with its modern operation. Ballard notes the shifty response.

Sir Harry hardly seems to have benefited from having passed the night in the guest house that was constructed for his use and furnished with a featherbed and brass lavatory fittings. Through fatigue-rimmed eyes he looks at the ascension balloon with disgust, as if it's yet another device designed primarily for his discomfort. Ballard asks if he would prefer to remain in camp.

"No, I'll do it," he says through gritted teeth.

The balloon's shadow dances among the dunes. Some inexplicably idle fellahin observe the party from a distance, their expressions passive, as if Montgolfiers are common desert flora. The pilot welcomes the Khedive, Sir Harry, Ballard, Thayer, and Miss Keaton onto the gondola, which hovers inches off the ground, its ballast bags loaded with sand—imported from Britain with the gondola. The vehicle rocks as it takes on the passengers' weight. Ballard briefly reflects, before an ascent hardly as dependable as a lift's, that it carries the four men essential to the Equilateral and the millions of pounds sterling that have been invested in it. Gripping the gondola's railing, the aeronauts wave to the onlookers, a small party of Europeans and the Khedive's entire entourage, including the military band, which performs "God Save the Queen" and the Egyptian national anthem, composed by Verdi.

The land they've been excavating suddenly drops away, accompanied by applause and hurrahs. Point A is far below at once.

As the sun-bleached tents and mud-brick structures of the settlement recede, Thayer murmurs surprise. In his carriage with Bint a few weeks ago, he thought he was circumnavigating a burgeoning metropolis. But very quickly now Point A is seen to be a modest desert outpost, a few hundred yards square, a cluster of tents and buildings, of which only the hammam and the pitch factory may be recognized.

Then the two sides of the triangle radiating from Point A come into view, diverging toward points beyond the horizon three hundred miles apart, two black, throbbing lines laid into the sand, just as foreseen in Thayer's letter to *Philosophical Transactions* in 1883, just as Ballard surveyed them in 1891 and '92. They cut through whatever dunes or hillocks they encounter. Their blackness imprints itself on Thayer's retinas. No one can doubt from this height or from any other that these are the artifacts of a sensitive, calculating intelligence. The balloon rises and the Equilateral continues to reveal itself.

The music from the Khedive's military band reaches them, with some of the instruments muted in the breeze and others amplified, producing exactly the sort of heavenly cry we may expect in the atmosphere's upper strata.

Exhilaration courses through Thayer's veins. He's impressed with even more force than he was at the pitch factory, when he saw little more than Vertex BAC, or when he stood on the ridge above Side AC. His eyes are wide, his mouth half open. All these years of hard labor are laid out below him on the alabaster plain as if on his own drafting table.

Without saying a word, Thayer takes Miss Keaton's warm right hand and squeezes it hard. For the next several minutes the secretary is unable to see the Equilateral, or the desert at all, or to hear the winds whistling through the lines that attach the gondola to the balloon. He releases his grip. When her vision clears and she can inspect the Equilateral below, she doesn't think of looking for the foreshortening of the triangle's upper portions in the far distance.

"My Lord Jesus."

At first Thayer believes it's Ballard who's whispered this gentle oath, but no, it's Sir Harry.

The few minutes aloft have wrought a transformation. Color has returned to his face. His mouth's twisted into an unguarded grin that's nearly boyish.

"My Lord Jesus," he repeats. "Look what we've brought off! This is the greatest mark of man's hand upon the Earth. Ballard, you've earned your place in history. Professor Thayer—" he begins, and then simply embraces him, almost overcome.

The Khedive is visibly moved as well, making lip-smacking noises and inward sighs. He lightly claps his hands.

"Bravo," he says. He releases a childish giggle.

Having taken out his pocket telescope, Thayer surveys the excavations. He follows each line below him, AC and AB, to its vanishing point. He removes his face from the glass to assure himself that the lines are actually there. They are! Thayer gazes at the figure for several minutes as their vessel sails farther into the thinning air, then, beaming, he turns to the unmarked, unmapped desert to the south. He anticipates additional, more complicated geometric figures beyond the ones planned for this decade. In the next century, they will dig a line that intersects two parallel lines, producing congruent angles; also, a circle with an inscribed angle half the size of a central angle subtending the same arc. Meanwhile, his companions continue to marvel at what their labor, their capital, and their viceregal writ have accomplished so far.

They marvel, yet Ballard intuits that something's amiss. He's stirred into an unfocused wariness that will, in short course, save the expedition from disaster.

With his glass raised again, Thayer examines the low line of hills on the southern horizon. Something arrests the instrument's drift. He peers at the hills with the intensity that he normally reserves for celestial observation. His mouth opens slightly. He closes down his other senses, even the internal commentaries and distractions that normally accompany thought, and bears down on the field of view.

"What do you see?" the Khedive asks.

Ballard and Miss Keaton follow the line of the glass to the horizon, they don't see anything, and they turn back to the astronomer.

Thayer is straining now, his eyes narrow, his jaw set hard as he studies the distant hills. But Ballard is the one who observes something definite—a deadly, silvery flash—right on board the gondola.

The engineer lunges at it, but the weapon strikes the Khedive first.

In a moment Ballard is wrestling on the narrow deck with the pilot, his hands gripping the wrist that holds the knife, whose cruel arc ends in a black ivory handle. There are cries and shouts and Thayer drops his glass against the rail, shattering the lens. Then the Khedive, uncowed by the attack, falls on the would-be assassin, pins him, and puts his knee hard against his windpipe. The man loses the knife and Miss Keaton kicks it away. Thayer and Sir Harry, who have stood back from the scuffle, cut lengths of mooring rope with the relinquished blade. They truss the man like a game fowl, even as he issues a series of imprecations.

But the Khedive is hardly finished.

He questions him severely in Arabic, apparently demanding to know his cause and his patron. The pilot responds with taunts that, Thayer gathers, impugns the honor of the Egyptian royal family, including by name the late Khedive Tewfik. This abuse enrages the son, who puts the knife to his throat. The bound man writhes in rebellion.

When the Khedive jerks him from the deck, the gondola shifts precipitously. As Thayer falls forward and grabs a guy wire supporting the basket, there's nothing between him and the Equilateral, which is laid out in front of him, quite close it seems, like his destiny. The Khedive inclines the pilot over the rail.

"Your Highness!" Sir Harry cries.

But the Khedive knows no inhibition. With a strength infused by his righteous anger at the insult to Mehmet Ali's royal line, which has governed Egypt for ninety years, he hauls the man over the railing, holding him by the ropes. The prisoner has been cut by his own knife. Blood freely runs down his face and uniform, but of more immediate concern to the dangling wretch is the obduracy of the African continent, thousands of feet below.

This threat proves remedial. Fear is lit in the villain's eyes as he apprehends his situation, which is made even more intolerable by the immobility of his hands, arms, and feet. When the Khedive poses the question again, the man responds—if not with complete civility, for terror has gained command over his composure, then at least usefully. The Khedive is sobered by the information imparted. A spasm of concern roils his forehead. He asks the man another question with evident urgency.

The Khedive is sufficiently satisfied by the man's response to return him to the gondola, so that he can be further interviewed by the police. But he proves to be an unwieldy package. As the Khedive pulls him in, the prisoner slips from his grasp.

Suddenly lightened, the balloon rockets heavenward. Sir Harry falls to the floor of the gondola, but the others grab the rail and watch the man drop, turning over and over, still bound. The vessel is now soaring above the southwest interior of the excavations. As the traitor silently plummets, and more seconds seem to pass than is possible, he shrinks in apparent size until, the Equilateral rushing to meet him, he becomes no more than that which is without parts, a single-dimensional element, a position but no magnitude—in other words, a point. Given that Egyptian methods of extracting information would blanch a Turk, his fall is a certain mercy.

"Professor Thayer," the khedive says, once the balloon stabilizes at its new altitude, about seven thousand feet. "I trust that your expertise in the arts and sciences encompasses the piloting of ascension balloons."

Thayer is in no position to confess that this is his first aeronautical expedition, as either operator or passenger. He consults with Ballard quietly on the use of the gas valve above the gondola, and together they make the adjustments necessary to descend comfortably. Employing the distinct, gentle breezes that prevail at each altitude, they reach the ground not far from Point A.

△

A military detachment rides out at a hard gallop. The Khedive's bodyguards saw from below that something sinister was transpiring on board the gondola and when they witnessed the body plunge into the desert wastes, they expected the worst. They cheer when they're met by the beaming Khedive, refreshed by his tussle with the treacherous pilot.

Not until then does anyone remark that the Khedive's tunic is sliced open across his chest, probably by the villain's initial parry. While his commanders voice consternation, the Khedive, who has already shown his royal mettle, coolly proceeds to unbutton his uniform.

The knife has gone clear through his tunic and undergarments, but when these are removed his corpulence shows itself unpunctured. The skin's marked only by a pale pink scratch that runs the full length of the blade's course, from nipple to umbilicus. It's as straight a line as anything conceived by Euclid.

△

Thayer is puzzled by the attack on the Khedive. Once they've returned to Point A, he asks Ballard if he believes the Mahdists are responsible.

"They're adamantly opposed to Egypt's rule in the Sudan," Ballard notes. "They despise the Khedive—as a tool of the

British, for his Albanian blood, for his palaces, for his yachts, and for his harem girls. Fair enough, I suppose. He's bold to come this far south, and damn foolish. But the assassin was not sent by the Mahdists at all."

"Then . . . ?"

"The Sublime Porte has never reconciled itself to the Equilateral."

"But I went to Constantinople! I met with the Sultan. I gave him sketches of Mars, showing the canals definitively. He expressed enormous enthusiasm."

"The Turks are masters of dissimulation," Ballard says. "Rather than play a losing hand, they switch the deck."

Unable to overtly resist the Concession, the Ottoman Sultan fears the Equilateral as yet another European scheme to wrest Egypt from his increasingly feeble grip. The Khedive's elimination would have jeopardized the project and sent Egypt into more than its usual turmoil. Yet the Mahdists would have been the ones to profit, so, Ballard concedes, perhaps Thayer's original supposition is correct.

The engineer asks Thayer what he observed through his pocket telescope.

"Nothing, really."

"Reticence doesn't become you, Thayer. Before that bit of unpleasantness with the pilot, you were looking at a definite position on the ground."

Thayer turns to gaze across the desert. He finds the approximate place, staring at it for a while, but without the advantage of elevation.

"There was motion of some kind," he says at last. "I think

that's what it was, motion, not a distinguishable object. Motion in the desert always catches the eye. This was on the horizon, a disturbance, a boiling, or something like the seething of a hive. I don't know. I saw it for only a moment and then I was jostled and I lost my glass." He adds, "Now, thank you, I have to send to London for its replacement."

TWENTY-FIVE

They never learn the particulars of the turncoat's confession, but his concluding statement is enough to bring about a series of arrests. Men are taken away. A Nubian corporal surrenders unprompted. Two bodyguards suddenly turn on a third, putting him in irons. Complementary actions are taken within the Khedive's palace in Cairo. The seizures seem entirely at random, or according to occult principles. The assault on the viceroy's life may have involved the Sublime Porte, and it may have involved the Mahdists, and it must be part of a larger scheme, but whatever it is, the conspiracy operates below the plane of the Equilateral. It recalls to the Europeans that they sojourn in Byzantine lands.

Because the lands are Byzantine, the evening's royal banquet unfolds as scheduled, with the scheduled extravagance: slaughtered goats, martyred lambs, mountains of rice, towers of figs and dates, a panoply of jellies and sauces, and rolling blue cumuli of hashish smoke. The bagnio girls have joined their sisters from the Khedive's harem for the night. Decked out in new raiments, hennaed, rouged, and bangled, they've been imparted with fresh glamour. They're pillowed at the table with the Khedive and his European companions, and they encourage and amplify the party's ribald humor. The Cairo haremites seem less worldly, but perhaps even more enticing for their pretensions to lustrous innocence. A wizened musician picks at a qanoon. Miss Keaton has of course absented herself.

Thayer is considerably more troubled by the attack than the Khedive appears to be, and even Sir Harry seems to have recovered his composure. The astronomer ignores the girls and eats little. No one speaks of the arrests. The two visitors to Point A lean across their plates to share a private observation. Sir Harry snorts in amused contempt. Thayer recognizes that he doesn't know every arrangement that has been made between the Khedive and the Concession. Not every appendix and codicil has been made public. The machinery of world politics turns invisibly. The ties of blood, clan, sect, and military obedience that maintain the Khedive's rule, and parallel ligatures bound in opposition to it, lie beyond Thayer's comprehension.

His early departure is hardly remarked. The day has taken much from him. When he arrives at his quarters, Bint has already left. He performs his own toilet and puts himself to bed, winning no more than an uneasy slumber that's roiled by visions of flashing knives and men plummeting into geometric figures.

△

Waking fevered in a darkened tent, Thayer calls for Bint. Another attendant appears. She comes at once, deferential and comely.

"Where's Bint?" he asks, the question a parched croak.

She smiles modestly and says, "Bint."

The girl looks very much like Bint, with the olive skin and almond eyes characteristic of the Near East's women. As a rule, males and females of the Eastern races do not display the variety of physical characteristics that distinguish individuals among the Europeans. Compare, say, Miss Sarah Bernhardt with Miss Eleonora Duse; both lovely and talented, yet as different in appearance from each other as the ocean and the sky (with the tempestuous Divine Sarah being the ocean, of course). Thayer can't be blamed for confusing the identities of two ordinary Arab serving girls.

"Yes, I need Bint," he says. "Please send her to me."

"Bint," she repeats. She pours water from an earthenware pitcher and offers him the cup.

Knowing that he's ill and that fever can cloud his perceptions, and also because he's a man of open mind, Thayer wonders if he's mistaken, and if this is indeed the girl who has been taking care of his domestic needs for more than a year. Especially after the turmoil of the previous day, he can be mistaken. He considers the familiarity of her features and mannerisms: the prow-like nose, the wide-eyed stare; she leans forward when she speaks, raising an arm as if in defense.

"You're not Bint," he declares. "Bint! Are you here?"

He struggles to stand and, still in his nightgown, he pulls open the entrance to the tent.

The shock of light and heat, accompanied by waves of nausea and vertigo, drives him back at once. Aware of his frailty, the girl gently takes him by the shoulders and brings him to his chair. He can't have expected more tenderness from anyone, not even from Bint.

△

Despite the girl's protestations, which are in the same key as Bint's and similarly unintelligible, Thayer dresses himself and goes out to Miss Keaton's bureau. She's behind her typewriter.

"What happened to Bint?"

"Good morning, are you all right?" She gets up from her desk. "You look ghastly."

"Bint's not in my tent. Some other girl is there. She calls herself Bint but she's not."

"That's odd," she agrees briskly. She studies him, worried. He's flushed now and his eyes are red. "How late did you remain at the banquet? Dr. McKinnon told you not to overindulge. Do you have a fever?"

"You didn't send her away?"

He stares at her intently, as if her most minute features, some so minute they border on the invisible, may betray the most vitally important truths.

"No, I wouldn't do that. I would ask you before I did, but I'm sufficiently occupied with the Equilateral! We still have men excavating Side AB. I'm calling for the doctor. If the fever has returned—"

"You didn't send her away?" he repeats.

She stops to consider the question. She can ask him why he thinks she would send her away, but his only possible response will humiliate her. All this, over an Arab serving girl . . . To think he believes that she would . . . She's dismayed, and then angry. He stands before her, waiting for her to confirm his suspicions. Her anger is dulled when she recalls the shortened sides. Before she can speak, before she can formulate the single correct series of words that will make him *see*, he rushes from the bureau.

△

Thayer soon loses his way to the women's dormitory, encountering unexpected lanes and alleys, before finding himself at the door to the tea room. This is where the jingle of female laughter was heard several months earlier.

Gazing off into space with a melancholic aspect redolent of the East, the Turk is in his accustomed place behind the counter. He's surprised to see anyone at this hour, especially the astronomer.

Thayer says, "I'm looking for Bint."

Daoud Pasha fingers his mustache and casts his eyes down, in feigned obsequiousness.

"You have a girl, Effendi. Do you wish a second?"

"No, I want Bint."

Now the Turk, letting go of his mustache, looks sharply at Thayer.

"Which girl?"

"Bint, my attendant. She's been with me for more than a year."

The Turk's manner turns gentle. His experience with Europeans extends back to the middle of the century, so he's not surprised by Thayer's error.

"That was Alya, Your Honor."

"No, the girl's name is Bint. Bint. You know her, you sent her to me."

"*Bint*," Daoud Pasha says. "That's the word for 'girl' in Arabic. Your former attendant's name is Alya. Your new attendant's name is Wadha. If you prefer, I can send you Noora. She's especially lovely, in her way. You can call her Bint too."

"Her name's not Alya," Thayer insists. "Her name is Bint."

"Every girl is a *bint*. Your mother is a *bint*. My mother is a *bint*. I have a *bint* for a wife, and Allah in His infinite wisdom has blessed me with four *bints*. And so it is written." He repeats, "*Bint* is the word for 'girl.'"

Thayer demands, "Where is she?"

"She's safe. She's not involved."

"With the attack on the Khedive? I'm sure she had nothing to do with it!"

"Certainly not, Effendi Professor."

The police have thoroughly investigated the assassination attempt. They've discovered certain stratagems, deceits, maneuvers, and intrigues within plots within conspiracies. A network of faint lines has become momentarily visible. Daoud Pasha explains that one of the conspirators is a member of the Zeygerat Tribe, which is related in marriage and occasional warfare to Alya's people, the Djebel Shammar. Members of both tribes are being returned to their villages. This is by order of the Khedive, who left for Cairo with Sir Harry in the cool of the night, after the banquet.

"I need her back."

"You fancy her, Effendi?"

"I've been ill," Thayer murmurs. "The Equilateral must be finished . . ."

△

Thayer wanders through the settlement, blinded by the sun, always the sun, and his personal, internal fever. The suppression of the conspiracy has replaced many of the familiar fellahin with other, stranger men; it has also shifted the direction of some alleyways and the location of the souk. All the tents appear alike. He can no longer separate the specific from the general. His boots guide him back to his quarters or what he believes are his quarters.

Bint's there, of course, to relieve him of the heat, accepting as much of it as she can on his behalf. She's alone in the darkened room, holding the pitcher and a towel to be used for a compress. But this is not the Bint he knew, who is being returned to her village. Yet this is *not* the Bint who was there earlier this morning. She has been replaced again. The Bints are endless, each a subtle variation on the other, a difference in the gaze, the bearing, the architecture of her cheekbones, or the set of her mouth. But this Bint, he is certain, is the nearest possible reproduction of the Bint who observed the new excavations in the Hellas Basin.

"Alya," Thayer says, speaking her name for the first time. He too is the nearest possible reproduction.

TWENTY-SIX

As Earth ascends in Mars' western sky from night to night, Martian astronomers intensify their debates about the regular scorings visible on a section of the third planet's dry lands. They note that the gaps in what appears to be an equal-sided triangle low in the northern temperate zone may be closing up just as the object reaches its farthest distance in the sky from the sun. This can't be a coincidence. Telescopes usually occupied with planet five and the ringed sixth swivel in our direction.

The Equilateral approaches completion—a miracle, except for those who know the toil it has extracted from its builders. Even now the paving is being thwarted by another accident in the Point A pitch factory, obstructions in transporting the oil, and difficulties in handling it. Ballard makes threats and offers bribes. The European press calls him the greatest engineer of the century.

Ballard accepts the praise; this is the culmination of his career in civil works, a construction that ranks as a modern wonder of the world. His satisfaction allows him to ignore rumors of further unrest in the Sudan, where the usual clerical fanatics rule that the Equilateral stands contrary to Mohammedan principles, whatever they may be. Ballard doesn't trouble himself with the grievance-laden text delivered by his spies; it's the usual grievances. He is, however, aware that the long-promised campaign against the Mahdists in Omdurman has failed to materialize. Those troops seen disembarking at Alexandria were apparently a mirage. Perhaps if Ballard had spoken with Thayer about the reports of poisoned wells, stolen camels, and villages annihilated in the dead of night, they would have connected them with the movements on the horizon that the astronomer detected from his perch in the balloon. Measures could have been taken.

But with little more than a week left before maximum elongation, Ballard is occupied with his final drive to victory— victory over the desert, victory over the smallness of men's ambitions, and victory over men's frailties and fears. He receives an influx of fellahin fresh from villages in North Africa, as distant as Morocco. They're immediately dispatched to the unfinished sections of Side AB, where they're given spades that have already excavated thousands of cubic yards. Hourly reports detail the final tests of the petroleum pipeline. The taps will be opened three days before maximum elongation, the amount of time required for the petroleum to occupy to a depth of twelve inches the paved, impermeable surface of the figure.

The engineers are already executing their plans to dismantle Point A, or at least to remove its salvageable artifacts: the light machinery, the water tankers, the hand tools, the tents, the surplus grain, and the livestock. The Europeans are also preparing to remove themselves. The project will end directly after the Flare is ignited early in the morning of June the seventeenth. As he reviews the evacuation schedule, Ballard sees that Miss Keaton has booked three passages from Alexandria to Marseilles.

Despite the numerous engineering challenges that occupy him today, Ballard makes time to stop at Thayer's tent. The astronomer is at his desk, studying Professor France-Lanord's latest observations of Mars, which have just arrived. The girl is absent.

"I trust you bring good news, Ballard. News as good as this, at least." He taps the sketches. "The growth of vegetation in the Hellas Basin has intensified since the equinox. The southern hemisphere harvest should meet their expectations."

"Then engineers have won victory on two worlds. The Equilateral is almost done. The petroleum is about to flow. Some excavation is still under way on Side AB, between miles eighty and one hundred, but we're close."

"How close?"

"Very," Ballard assures him. In fact a dune field lies between the completed segments. Thousands of men are hacking through it from each side, but they remain miles apart. They'll still be digging in the hours before the Flare is ignited.

"And the pitch?"

"Laid down, nearly everywhere. And then, after the Flare, we'll be good and done. I'm looking forward to seeing civilization again! Provisions have been made for returning the fellahin to their villages. The Nubians will go back to their armies. Every person will be restored to his proper place, or hers."

Thayer doesn't acknowledge the suggestion. Ballard gives him another moment and then adds:

"My advice is to make a clean break of it."

The astronomer returns to France-Lanord's sketches.

Ballard says, "You've taken on responsibility for the girl, based on chivalric ideals not shared by the Arabs or even known to them. According to local custom the girl was ruined long ago, losing the protection of her fathers and brothers—otherwise she would have never come to Point A. But she'll never be received as your companion in England. It's not possible for you to live there together. Allowing the attachment to linger will make the inevitable separation all the worse. I'm telling you this as a friend, Sanford."

The astronomer listens in silence, still as the sands. Then he says, "Have you tested the electrical igniters? The chronometers?"

"Yes, of course."

"Every section of the Equilateral must be lit simultaneously."

"I know," Ballard says. "Listen, this is hardly my affair, but sometimes what's hardest to make out is right there . . . You may not be aware that someone cares for you. You may not observe that it's someone you care for in the only way that is proper. Someone who possesses many admirable qualities with whom you can share a life in England or anywhere else in the world. You know of whom I speak."

"I don't," Thayer murmurs.

△

After Ballard leaves, Thayer falls into a kind of trance, similar to and perhaps indistinguishable from a fever-induced stupor.

As is often the case when he appears insensible to his surroundings, his mind is working with great vigor.

When Miss Keaton stops in, he instructs her to make the arrangements to return Bint to her village. Taking notes, the secretary displays no emotion. She herself is not sure how she feels; or rather, she is keenly aware of her relief and elation, and at the same time she senses Thayer's regret and suffers for it.

Thayer says, "Don't let on that you're doing this, but deposit some extra money into her account. A few hundred pounds."

"All right. I can do that."

"No one will marry her, you know."

"No, no one will," Miss Keaton agrees sadly. She recognizes that in this part of the world an unmarried woman is a manifest tragedy: shunned, impoverished, unprotected, purposeless, and as lonely as a planet without its star. She abstains from extending this observation.

TWENTY-SEVEN

The rocky red runner sprints toward June the seventeenth, rising earlier every night. Ares burns in the constellation Aquarius; so does Merrikh, Nergal, Pyroeis, Angaraka, Ma'adim. Point A's atmosphere is steeped in volatiles as petroleum is pumped into the excavated figure. We should have known the planet's sanguineous rays meant war.

During the hours of the night when the fifteenth becomes the sixteenth, the night before maximum elongation, the pumping of the petroleum proceeds close to schedule, the greatest transport of liquid substance in the history of civilization, through a system of conduits twice the length of the Roman aqueducts at their maximum extent. Teams of riders patrol the pipeline, checking for leaks. If any occur, engineers stand by at dozens of designated sites, prepared to seal them.

Already Point A is taking on the chill of abandonment, like a resort out of season (if either the words *chill* or *resort* can be employed as similes anywhere within the baked flats of the Western Desert). The evacuation has begun, many of the fellahin paid, dismissed, and conveyed home. Whole neighborhoods are silently dismantled, leaving the sand as unblemished as if it has never been inhabited at all.

Damp whispers warn of shadows moving between tents. Ballard doesn't necessarily credit these reports as true, knowing that his informants are prone to night terrors and extravagant noonday speculation, but he knows too that the number of informants is dwindling.

The imminence of maximum elongation has returned him to his customary alertness. He stays awake that night while two ancient spheres wheel along indelibly grooved tracks. Petroleum mist precipitates into his lungs. The hyenas that prowl the middens fall into speechless meditation. At around eleven the engineer checks that his guns are loaded, takes his best, the Martini-Henry with which he once brought down a leopard, and steps from his tent.

Point A is hushed. Other men lie awake in their camp beds, attending the silence and wondering what the following night will bring, provided it comes. Mars hasn't risen yet. Saturn, Cronus, stares cold and unblinking in the west. Ballard scans the horizon to the south. He will recall later that he saw something there, but that belief may be retroactive, influenced by the following events.

△

The military intelligence received from the Sudan neglects to mention that in the fiery dark eyes of the Mahdists the greatest insult to the Mohammedan faith is the pitch factory. Perhaps it's the building's kilned-brick construction that offends them, or there's some obscure non-Mohammedan feature in the tower's simple lines, or they believe it's a church; perhaps it's the bottomless blackness of the pitch itself. The grounds for their anger are unknowable, but it's a lucky stroke, because the Mahdists spend their initial fury on the structure, which is about to be abandoned anyway, giving the Europeans time to organize their defenses.

The Mahdists number about fifteen hundred rifles, the same size as Point A's military detachment, but they're faster, stronger, better shots, and better led, and fanatics besides. They've crept north from the Sudan in uncanny silence; they enter Point A in a thundering onslaught. In their furious drive at the factory, they discharge their weapons blindly, slaying European and native alike.

The Nubian guards are not entirely worthless, save for those who go over to the Mahdists. Their captain organizes a defensive cordon around the tea room, where the Europeans secure themselves.

Ballard rides out with the Nubians, seeking to bag a few of the invaders himself. It's a difficult skirmish, for there's little cover and the Mahdists are practiced in desert warfare, as the Concession's force is not. Having wrecked the pitch factory, the Mahdists proceed to attack the hammam, the women's dormitory, the machine shop, and the administrative quarters. A single clapboard building, foreign and enigmatic, is left untouched. Bombs fly. Ballard takes his shots carefully, noting with approval whenever another mount flees riderless from the melee.

The Europeans mill within the tea room. Daoud Pasha has disappeared from his post behind the bar. A few of the men itch to join the fight, but most are scientists and engineers who have never seen combat. They shudder at every shot, shout, and cry outside.

Thayer stands in the tea room with Miss Keaton, apart from their colleagues. She doesn't speak, showing admirable sang-froid, and perhaps more confidence in the Nubians than is warranted. Thayer's response to the assault, the largest Mahdist action staged in North Africa since Khartoum, is characterized initially by peevishness. He grimaces at every rifle's report. He mutters, "Idiots," to no one in particular. As the fighting around the tearoom intensifies, his annoyance is replaced by disquiet. Then he falls into a daze, as if to deny the violence beyond the room's walls, through which bullets occasionally pass. It lasts until the instant when Miss Keaton cries out and he tears from the tea room unarmed.

Ballard catches sight of him briefly, before being set upon by a Mahdist with a jeweled cutlass, as the astronomer runs with his head down across the field of battle, where the cries of men killing and dying, the womanish moans of falling camels, and the sweet stench of the petroleum are at their most powerful. Allah's being beseeched; also, in some quarters, no less urgently, is our Savior. Now purposing their fire fully on the destruction of the Concession's troops, the raiders push them back toward the Vertex, over which a black pool of oil spills several miles wide. In the dark of the night fumes refract the starshine. Dispatching the Arab, Ballard reflects that he's been in scrapes worse than this, but not much worse.

The single man responsible for Christianity's greatest affront to Islam (since the previous), Thayer goes unseen by the

Mahdists as he sprints to the female quarters. He dashes among the girls who have fled the building. They've been reduced to insensate terror. Some wail and beat their chests.

The weather station in Alexandria fixes this moment within the thirty-sixth minute past the twenty-third hour at the local meridian, later corroborating it with observations from Royal Navy ships off the Egyptian coast, as well as with several stopped clocks that will be found among the debris. In this moment one of the Mahdists, or perhaps one of the Nubians, flings a torch at the combatants. Ballard sees it himself as it arcs through the dense, mephitic air, and he knows then that the terms of the contest are about to be radically altered.

In that same capacious instant, short of twenty-three hours, thirty-six minutes, fourteen seconds only by the duration of the missile's flight, Thayer discovers Bint, not outside the dormitory, which he never reaches, but near the remains of the hammam. Unlike the other Arab girls stranded on the battlefield, she doesn't cower in terror. On the contrary, she stands serene, observing the warfare as if it's elsewhere, someplace distant. She's wrapped in her crimson shawl. When the astronomer descends from the tumult she allows him her usual small shy smile. He makes her no acknowledgment, charging across the sand like a locomotive, and when he reaches her he puts his arms around her diminutive torso, the first time they've embraced, and he hurls her to the sand. She cries in surprise. He smothers her body with his.

Elaborate precautions, approved by the Concession, have been observed throughout the pumping of the petroleum. Ballard knew, of course, that the atmosphere, saturated with hydrocarbons, would become flammable. He has accurately predicted the local effects of the Flare and he put into place safety measures to be performed during the Equilateral's illumination. The signal to Mars was to have been ignited by multiple electrical charges after his personnel were removed to a safe distance. As he will later declare to the Parliamentary committee, he could never have foreseen the ignorance and recklessness of the Mahdists.

The pool ignites, either in direct contact with the missile or because the air has become inflamed. The first sound is a kind of thump, like a tremendous chest falling from a tremendous wagon, followed by a hissing, hushing roar. In a moment Point A is more brightly lit than it is at brutal noon, as if another sun has risen from the Vertex. The figures of the men are rendered no less two-dimensional than their looming, knife-edged shadows. A screaming wall of flame streaks across the desert along Sides AB and AC, jumping the gaps, toward the Equilateral's other two oil-filled vertices.

Toward the eastern end of the Equilateral, on Side AB, where the men are still excavating the dunes and laying pitch, taking advantage of the cooler nighttime temperatures, some witness the oncoming rush of predatory light, but they're unable to run for safety. Thousands of fellahin perish at once and thousands more receive burns too serious to be treated. Once the vertices at Point B and Point C catch fire, the fatal rays are straight-ruled along Side BC, where they meet at its midpoint; call it Point I. Incendiary scraps of matter, mostly canvas and flesh, rise in the fire's draft. Roosters in villages on the Nile greet the man-made dawn. Ships in the Mediterranean observe the unnatural glow, which is recorded as far away as Palermo. The Flare is fully lit, but the Earth's spin has not yet brought Egypt into the view of Mars. The signal instead flashes out to the distant stars, whose astronomers will debate what it means centuries hence.

At Point A most of the immediate casualties lie near the edge of the Vertex, where they're engulfed in the conflagration. Ballard leaps off his horse and goes to the ground with his rifle. He keeps it cocked as he watches men with their bodies inflamed roll in the sand, crying for help. The bakery is on fire too, as is nearly every other structure attacked by the Mahdists. Ballard believes he's safe, but he hasn't reckoned on the blaze's appetite for oxygen.

He witnesses the effects on other men first: they clutch their throats. As his lungs fill with the products of combustion, he's soon compelled to do the same.

He blacks out, either for a moment or for a few minutes.

△

When he recovers, the chief engineer finds himself transported to a crepuscular landscape of abject desolation, surrounded by the stinking, smoking, charred remains of men, camels, and horses, lit orange by the subsiding flames. Flickering, living shadows play among the dunes. The other survivors are no less dazed than he is, with most of them unaware of how they've been scorched. They can no longer tell attacker from defender, and in the aftermath they can't recall why they are there or the nature of the prize they have so savagely contested.

Point A is silenced now. A dense brimstone haze hangs over

the settlement. Ballard picks himself up and, with his rifle lowered, he returns to the still-standing tea room, from which his
colleagues emerge intact, looking about in hushed wonder.
Thayer isn't among them. But the Earth continues to turn and
once North Africa comes around, Mars will observe the Equilateral all but completed, a figure some thinking mind has carved
and burned into the surface of the terraqueous third planet.

TWENTY-EIGHT

News of the Equilateral's realization grips the capitals of Europe with the force of a royal engagement or the threat of war. The Sunday supplements populate continents of newsprint with firsthand accounts of the desert excavations, the Mahdist attack on Point A, and the premature ignition of the Flare. Telescopes great and small turn again to the Red Planet, which steadily draws near. Professional astronomers cable long descriptive letters to the papers. Astronomy is taken up by leisured gentlemen, who compete to provide their friends with the freshest and most revealing sketches of the planet's surface.

Returning to London, Ballard is honored at a Downing Street banquet by the prime minister, the Earl of Rosebery, who speaks of his pride in the Equilateral and his tempered regret for the failure of the Flare. He himself has installed a six-inch Newtonian refractor at his estate in Mentmore. Ballard soaks in the glory, which is so abundant that there is more than enough to share with Thayer. The astronomer's likeness is in every newspaper, on posters in shop windows, on biscuit tins, on candy boxes, on soap boxes, and on the covers of biographies rushed into print, usually accompanied by the illustration of an equal-sided triangle. The Royal Astronomical Society names after Thayer a newly discovered minor planet that travels within the orbits of Earth and Mars, but nearer to Mars. Buckingham Palace has set into motion the mechanisms that will generate a peerage.

The Flare's undoing is not lost on anyone, but we allow it to diminish neither our spirits nor our expectations. The compromise of Thayer's designs truly reflects the division of our world, between progress and reaction, and between light and dark. Every misadventure reminds us against what we struggle.

△

The hyenas have returned to 25 degrees 40' 26" north latitude, 25 degrees 10' 6" east longitude. They nose in the sands for buried refuse, of which there is too much to fight over. They've grown lazy, especially after the few Europeans who remain at Point A stopped shooting at them. The settlement's inhabitants have consolidated their quarters into a single defensible outpost and are satisfied to watch the surrounding heaps of ash, bricks, and rubbish be buried by sand or blown away. Nomads have taken some of the light unusable equipment, as well as many of the oddly shaped pieces of crystal that the fire forged from the sands. The glass inexhaustibly splashed around the Vertex—twisted pillars, glowing beads, chamber-riddled boulders, translucent cylinders, glittering rhombohedrons, purple, pink, and green—will become an enduring component of the Near East's folk art. Equilaterals, they're called. The men give the hyenas wide berth and avoid more intercourse than is necessary with the two silent, hooded figures that dwell in the site's shadows.

When the Flare was ignited, one of the accompanying fire-balls engulfed Thayer and the Bedouin girl. Immersed in light, they were nuzzled and licked by the flames and were rocked by its updrafts. They held tight. They sucked in the sweet, rarefied air and found something cool and emollient in the core of the holocaust. After the fire extinguished itself and the settlement fell quiet, save for the strangled cries of the dying, the astronomer and the girl rose from the vitrified sand stripped of every article of clothing, their skin glowing pink. The scouring fire had reduced them to a state of nature. Even though they were unharmed, their figures were markedly altered. Their skulls were smoothly bald and every hair, every eyebrow, every cilium, and each pubic tuft were removed from their bodies. Not a single strand will grow back. They observed their hairlessness with wonder, as if truly seeing each other for the first time.

Miss Keaton came out of the tea room shaken but intact, looking for Thayer and knowing he'd be found with the girl. She remarked their nakedness and discovered that she expected that too. In the next few weeks, with help from the Europeans and the fellahin left at Point A, she assembled new quarters for the astronomer, whose desk, notebooks, sketches, calculations, and maps of Mars were destroyed in the attack. They traded with passing caravans for their coarse cotton robes, a white galabiya for Thayer and a new crimson robe for the girl. Before taking his leave, Ballard ensured that the line to Alexandria was restored. Miss Keaton now operates the cable equipment herself, occupying nearly every daylight hour in the telegraphic bureau, attentive to every jot and dash pouring in from distant lands. She dispatches her own in return, at great length.

Daoud Pasha is gone, either abducted or incinerated or as rich as Croesus: the Concession's historians will discover vast, astronomical inconsistencies in the tea room accounts. As for the girl, she has remained no less a mercurial, spectral presence than she was before, attending Thayer while he studies the new cables and manipulates figures on scraps of precious foolscap. She continues to bring him his tea. He smiles absently and sometimes when she's not there he picks up his smooth, highly reflective head to listen for her approach.

Miss Keaton accepts that they will not be returning to Cambridgeshire after all. She recognizes, reluctantly and painfully, that she has entertained a series of vague expectations about what would happen once the Equilateral was completed, and what her life with Thayer would be like once their years of toil and privation were behind them. She was of course hideously mistaken. A return to England, even at this hour of the Equilateral's accomplishment, can provide only further reminders of her error. The sterile, static desert comforts her in the daytime; the sky, as always, relieves her at night.

In any case, the correspondence now arrives in a torrent, with open-ended questions and tentative, unreliable answers about what is being seen on the ever-closer Martian surface. Government ministers, newspapermen, the Concession's governors, and the world's public await the Red Planet's response to the Equilateral, which they expect even though the Flare has gone unseen. Miss Keaton must continuously consult with Thayer, while the girl hardly leaves his side and their robes and common baldness set them apart. With Miss Keaton, Thayer expresses in precise, professorial language the apparent complexities of planetary motion, the varying illumination of distant celestial bodies, relative atmospheric conditions, and the vagaries of human eyesight; when he turns to the girl, he manages to communicate what's necessary with subvocal murmurs and primitive gestures.

Thayer initially seems revitalized by the Equilateral's completion—he doesn't speak of the Flare—and then by the hosannahs that reach them on the Great Sand Sea. Yet Miss Keaton detects a certain weakness, an occasional palsy, and a moment of inattention or incomprehension when she addresses him. It's several weeks before she becomes accustomed to Thayer's hairlessness, as well as to the robe and the new, less penetrative cast of the blue eyes that radiate from the shadows of his white cowl. They're as bright and cool as ever, yet often they seem fixed on an object elsewhere. His hand takes a moment to find the teacup that she offers him. They don't speak of this either.

No, he can't speak of the Flare; he can hardly think of the events that led to the mistimed firing. Days of obscurity are followed by electric nights when Thayer believes the lighting of the petroleum still lies in the future. At other times the Earth remains fixed in its place in the sky of Mars, and the Flare continues to burn, casting on the fourth planet's sere sands the permanent shadow of man's greatest accomplishment.

△

One aspect of the attack on Point A unreported in the press is that the Mahdists spared the observatory, thoughtlessly sweeping past it. Only one of the men stopped. He dismounted, approached the building, and smashed the lock with an ax. He stepped inside the windowless shed, still breathing hard from his ride, and pondered the object in the murk. He circled around the cold steel barrel. He tentatively pressed a lever extending from above his head and was startled when the roof slid open. The stars were revealed in a rush, and he knew that the machine was not a gun. Embarrassed by his fright, he realized then that it was not a weapon at all, but something utterly foreign, directly connected to something in the infinite. Unsettled by the encounter, he left the shed open but didn't lay a hand on the instrument.

TWENTY-NINE

I n the long course of the unusually clear-skied summer, Earth continues to close the distance with Mars, which gets more intense scrutiny than it ever has before. New controversies erupt, in particular over the discovery of canals radiating from the Elysium Basin in the northern temperate zone, one apparently extending toward Mnemosyne, the other to Arcadia. Thayer's colleagues struggle to find France-Lanord's markings around Hellas, in the planet's more easily observed southern hemisphere.

Point A receives hourly bulletins from the Concession, which forwards detailed reports from the world's planetary astronomers. Their observations are often at odds with each other, entire networks of waterways being erased from one night to the next. Thayer fires back in reply, demanding that they look again for the features that he's identified, but he sadly expects them to fail. He knows the corresponding visual weaknesses and strengths of his colleagues: whose eyes are capable of resolving close double stars but are unable to recognize faint shadings or patterns on a planetary surface; whose eyes are easily blinded by a disk's full illumination; whose optic nerves are connected to brains of plodding imagination. He can very nearly predict which astronomer won't see what.

△

Mars is now seventeen seconds across, no more than a tiny fraction of the eyepiece's field of view, yet for Thayer it's enormous, five times its apparent size last October when it emerged from behind the sun. As always the planet is featureless upon immediate viewing, but the image is steady and the object shows itself to be a three-dimensional solid, almost graspable. It's a marble we can insert into our mouths, roll around on our tongues, taste, and take care not to swallow. He peers deeply into the ocher pit and, after a long while, a single phantom makes itself known, followed by the rumor of another. Thayer holds very still, save to caress the fine-motion screw centering the planet. The girl stands behind him and Miss Keaton stands behind her. Thayer murmurs something. Then he sharply takes in his breath. His eyes never leave the eyepiece. His lower lip trembles.

The markings at Peneus, almost in the center of the disk, have been extended on either side, from Hellespontus to Malea. But the regions bordering the excavations have not deepened their shades and become verdant, as is usually the case with the canals at springtime. Another line is also becoming apparent, from Hellespontus to the Hellas Basin, completing the figure.

The bald, hooded man shudders and exhales.

KEN KALFUS

"It's very clear," he announces when he finally pulls away from the eyepiece. He speaks to both women, though only one may understand. "This is the most important discovery yet. Now we know what they're constructing north of Mare Australe. Those aren't canals. No one constructs a triangular canal. It's obvious. They've responded to our Equilateral by excavating their own, conveniently situated to be observed from Earth!"

"A triangle . . ." Miss Keaton murmurs, trying to make herself recognize the implications, even though what she is most aware of is that Thayer has stepped away from the telescope to make way for the girl.

The bald, hooded girl again shows enormous patience at the eyepiece, before scratching a figure on the palm of her small, delicate hand. It's a triangle. She holds up her hand for both to see, as if the diagram will remain visible there.

At the eyepiece, Miss Keaton tries to approach the girl's stillness, but she finds herself distracted, in no position to peer through the murk of space at a faraway turning stone. Thayer's feature refuses to resolve itself. She thinks she may see the same new Hellas canal they observed in May, but she's not even sure of that.

When she finally pulls back from the telescope, Thayer's watches her intently, waiting for confirmation. Offering confirmation will be much easier than withholding it, and also the best thing for Thayer's precarious health. But Miss Keaton finds herself rebelling against confirmation. She hasn't seen the triangle.

Thayer turns away, and wipes the absence of confirmation from his mind.

△

Miss Keaton cables Thayer's report to the Concession, which relays it to the International Astronomical Congress. No one will remark the absence of the second observer's name. The world's leading astronomers are notified.

Corroborations shortly flood the wires in return, from Professor Verzola in Padua, from Professor Belokovsky at Pulkovo near St. Petersburg, from Professor Barnard at Lick in California, and from Professor Max Wolf in Heidelberg. At the same time, as Thayer has anticipated, the skeptics who have opposed the Equilateral, calling him a fraud, now deny that the new markings are as regular as he claims. These are the men, now in the despised minority, who denied they saw canals even when they were made manifest in the world's greatest telescopes, in the best conditions. Thayer smirks as he reads their dissents.

"Fools," Miss Keaton agrees, but a keen observer would have noticed in the epithet a shimmer of a quaver.

"Blockheads," Thayer asserts.

Miss Keaton admires the skills of their European and American correspondents, and of course Sanford Thayer remains the world's keenest practitioner of the astronomical science and its attendant arts. Time and again Thayer has been the first man to see planetary features and starry phenomena that were later confirmed by his colleagues. Miss Keaton suspects that her inability to distinguish the Mars Equilateral lies within herself, and that this failure reflects a weakness more profound than a defect in her eyesight. She has never before failed to see what Thayer has discovered.

△

The International Astronomical Congress calls an extraordinary conference at the Royal Albert Hall, the greatest gathering of astronomers in history. They come to London, their suitcases bulging with reports and sketchbooks. They give interviews to the press and lectures to a paying, clamoring public. At midday we may walk into a cigar shop and overhear two gentlemen arguing declinations and hours of right ascension. The visitors erect their portable telescopes on every green at evening dusk.

Isolated at Point A, Thayer nevertheless enjoys his success. The cables report that many of his early opponents occupy the Hall. Having once regarded him as a charlatan, the best of them have been won over to the Equilateral's vital purpose by evidence and argument, the others by the accelerating prestige of Martian studies, which have brought opportunities for research sinecures and academic advancement. Thayer reads that as his colleagues filed into the Hall this morning, they shouted their huzzahs to him.

For three days the astronomers present their observations of the new markings in Hellas, confirming and amplifying Thayer's findings. The dozens of journalists who crowd the wings, smoking cigarettes, consider the reports dry and repetitive, but they abruptly lift their pens when Professor Hector France-Lanord presents what he says are the most definitive measurements of the figure's size. Several preceding speakers have noted that it appears to be larger than our own Equilateral. Without raising his voice, or showing any suggestion of satisfaction or enthusiasm, France-Lanord reveals that the Mars triangle is in fact 921 miles on a side, *precisely* three times as large.

The implications surge through the hall and spill onto the streets, where the newsboys are hawking special editions almost before he has returned to his seat. We're aware of the arduous human labor that has been required to dig the simple geometric figure Great Sand Sea. In order to excavate an Equilateral whose lines are three times as long, in a fraction of the time, Mars must possess a level of engineering expertise millennia beyond man's, just as we suspected. The newspapers illustrate steam-driven earth-moving equipment the size of cathedrals and an under-race of tireless, single-minded giants.

Yet the astronomers are made uneasy by the question of why the inhabitants of Mars have so fastidiously tripled the size of their Equilateral. The immediate speculation in the hall, on the streets, and in government ministries across Europe is that they're mocking the Concession's laborious progress across the Western Desert. They're acknowledging our primitive intelligence while simultaneously asserting their superiority. In any kind of social exchange, Earth will remain the subordinate partner. Some of the newspapers urge their governments not to accept any cut or condescension. One writer suggests that our neighbors' need to impress demonstrates a lack of confidence, which has been diminished by their accelerating senescence and their awe of man's virility.

In his cables to London, dictated to Miss Keaton, Thayer disputes these uninformed, hysterical interpretations, announcing that he's pleased, and indeed gratified, by the Hellas triangle's extent. As members of a younger race, the men of Earth will have much to learn from Mars, but our neighbors' prompt, enthusiastic response is rather a gesture of fellowship, and a promise that the wealth of Mars' civilization will be shared. If our Equilateral has been a sort of peace offering to the fourth planet, then the gift has been returned handsomely.

△

One moonless September night while Thayer and the girl sleep, and the entire camp at Point A is silent save for the unclassified, unknowable desert fauna, Miss Keaton unlocks the observatory. Mars rests at the edge of Aries, brighter than Sirius, already near minus-two magnitude. Phobos and Deimos spark from opposite sides of the planet, whose features gradually materialize. The south pole is soon visible, much smaller than it was before maximum elongation. The Hellas Basin has moved into the center of the disk, showing a certain brightness. Within Hellas, however, she detects only shifting shadows. Even now, as our world celebrates the discovery of an equilateral triangle drawn on the surface of another, she's unable to see the figure at all.

THIRTY

After months of almost hourly telegraphed observations, analysis, instructions, and arguments, the cable from Point A suddenly falls silent and the Earth's capitals are plunged into confusion. October the twelfth, the date of Mars' closest approach, is imminent. Unrequited appeals are sent back across the line. The Concession insists the telegraphic equipment is operating properly, but the newspapers declare that the lines must have been severed by the Mahdists, or very likely they have overrun Point A again and put Thayer himself to the torch. Sir Harry convenes with the ministers of the Great Powers to consider a military relief force.

Something is wrong indeed, but not with the telegraphic equipment. Thayer's been put to the torch by the resurgent fever; his metabolism's been overrun. No cool compress, no water splashed in his face, and no alcohol bath can bring down his temperature. The girl works with tight-lipped urgency. The astronomer is unconscious most of the time. When he's awake he insists that she allow light into the sickroom, which is already fully illuminated.

Miss Keaton stands by, ignoring the telegraphic signals that after traveling thousands of miles across Europe and the Mediterranean now spill onto the sands unread. The telegraph bureau has become a loathsome place, the locus of all points that encompass her sorrow. But even in Thayer's tent, the clatter of the cables reaches her ears, begging her to respond, expressing their own disappointment and fears.

The secretary is grateful for the girl's confident ministrations. When one treatment fails to bring Thayer's fever down, she swiftly employs another. The girl in turn recognizes Miss Keaton's wretchedness and offers her small tasks to perform for the sake of the patient: fetching water, boiling tea. Early one morning, as his temperature spikes again, the girl signals to Miss Keaton that she's leaving.

"Where are you going? Where?" Miss Keaton demands, alarmed.

The girl motions outside the tent, into the void.

"You can't go! He's burning up. What will I do?"

"Make sure he takes water. I'll return within the hour. He's very ill; Kharga Fever is very often fatal. If we don't do something now, it certainly will be."

"What are you saying?"

△

The girl's secret pharmacopoeia has been depleted, and the quarter in which the apothecary was located is gone, leaving only the faint scents of myrrh and galbanum, storax and onycha, coiling up from the sands. The fellahin who have remained at Point A, unwilling or unable to return to their villages, are disconcerted when she goes out among the settlement's ruins and presents herself at their dispersed quarters. Although she's fully dressed, her hairless brow reminds them of the nakedness beneath her robes, and also of her malign, shameful, obscure alliance with the astronomer. She demands whatever medicinal substances they may be hoarding.

From the raw ingredients she's collected, the girl prepares several potions and a gray, mustardy poultice. Miss Keaton doesn't object; the medical delegation left long ago. Gradually the fever abates. Thayer stirs. It's October the tenth, two days before Mars' closest approach.

They insist that he retire to his camp bed. The girl speaks urgently, fluently, rationally, affectionately, and eventually with anger; Miss Keaton says only, "Sanford!" Directly opposite the Earth from the sun, Mars rises now at evening dusk. Thayer insists that he must go to the observatory, even if it means staggering there, even if he nearly stumbles over his robe, even if Point A has taken on an unusually soft, fluid aspect that makes it difficult to find the structure, even if he's nearly too weak to pull the lever that slides open the roof. The two women stand behind him, united in their fury. Thayer takes some time before aligning his eye with the instrument.

But Mars is there, fully twenty-two arc seconds in diameter, as large as it will get this year. The planet has been waiting for him.

Furthermore, the seeing at Point A has improved beyond Thayer's expectations: a solid ten on the Douglass scale; no, it's gone beyond ten, the sky is darker, more transparent, more proximate than anyone ever thought possible, reminding us, yet again, that our planet whirls through the same vacuum ocean as any celestial object. Messier 33 and M34 are visible to the naked eye, bobbing space anemones. The Andromeda Nebula's a starry thumbprint smudged on the underside of the heavenly dome.

In the eyepiece, Mars hangs even more tangibly, more tantalizingly ripe than it did before his illness. Hellas is again well placed for observation, near the center of the planetary disk. The Equilateral and other features are immediately apparent. He sees at once that the southern cap has melted off half its volume, corresponding to the growth of the effervescently blue Syrtis Major sea.

Even as he gazes into the disk, other features develop: a possibly new waterway or causeway linking the Hammonis Cornu promontory to Hellas, and then a peculiar shadowing in Noachis, west of Hellas. Even more peculiar, there's something *outside* the disk, evidently in the thin upper atmosphere above Mare Australe. It's a line, a red-pink fluorescing line, that he has never seen before. None of us have.

"Two or three . . ." he murmurs to himself. "Faint, wispy tendrils. Red, pink, purple . . . Very high atmospheric phenomena . . . They're projections of some kind! That's what they are, coming off the disk, perhaps half the disk's radius, extending from about due south. Oh, my, oh, my! They're prominences . . ."

Thayer won't remove his eyes from the telescope or blink. He tracks the planet up and down the celestial bowl during the passage of the night, ignoring the girl's entreaties to rest. He doesn't invite his companions to view the planet; he doesn't seem aware of them. The atmospheric filaments hang above Mare Australe for hours, fading only as Mars sinks into the horizon near dawn.

The telegraph finally stutters to life at Mars House. Sir Harry is summoned at once. The staff cheers. Operating the Point A telegraphic equipment himself, Thayer doesn't report his illness, but the unacknowledged silence of the past ten days adds gravity and credence to the electrifying cable, punched on a continuous paper strip, that unwinds from the device in London.

That morning at Point A Thayer can't rest: he's too stimulated, too exhilarated, too far lost in a calculating reverie. The Concession demands a clarification. He cables back a clarification, as well as elaborations, arguments, presumptive refutations of any challenges, and telegraphic shouts of triumph. By the end of the day his colleagues in California, observing Mars hours after it has set in Egypt, confirm the prominences, even if they have not seen them in as great detail.

The new geometric figure on the surface of Mars is clearly not the only response to the excavations in the Western Desert. Clouds have risen into Mars' tenuous atmosphere. They're likely to be rich in carbon dioxide, nitrogen, sulfur, and several potassium compounds. The Concession's public statement draws no explicit conclusion, but its description of the phenomenon leaves the unavoidable impression of the smoky effluvia that typically accompanies the discharge of terrestrial cannon.

At dusk that evening, Thayer returns to the telescope and fails to observe Miss Keaton's deliberate absence. Yesterday's prominences are gone, save for a single nebulosity off the planet's surface, high above its south pole. The other filaments have vanished, just as we would expect from the gaseous by-products of combustion.

△

Is Earth under attack? An Oxford linguist suggests that among the inhabitants of Mars the display of an equal-sided triangle commonly represents a grave insult, or even a declaration of war. Mars' own, greater Equilateral, excavated in response to this interplanetary misunderstanding, indicates then a repetition and amplification of the aspersion, or an even more belligerent, less compromising acceptance of the military challenge. The papers cry that mortars have been fired from the Martian surface. Ministers secrete themselves in their offices late into the night, wondering how they will prepare their armies for celestial bombardment.

With the full weight of the Concession behind him, Thayer assures the world of Mars' peaceful intentions. He cables members of Parliament directly, explaining that the shells were launched without destructive force or intent. He has made precise measurements of the prominences. Judging from the size of the discharges and the peculiarities of the trails lingering in the Martian atmosphere, the projectiles are most likely several airtight vessels transporting, at this very moment, a diplomatic embassy across the forty million miles that separate the two planets, as heroic a voyage as any taken by Columbus or Magellan. Determining the velocity indicated by the dissipation of the cannon's fumes, Thayer predicts the fleet will make landfall on Earth within a matter of months, perhaps as early as July the first, 1895, just a year after maximum elongation. He declares that the vessels will arrive somewhere in Egypt and, almost certainly, that their landing place will be located in the vicinity of the geometric figure that has beckoned them to our planet, most logically at Point A.

THIRTY-ONE

Ballard is directed to construct the customs house. Erected on the sands formerly occupied by the wrecked pitch factory near Vertex BAC, the building will be hewn in majestic dimensions, greater than its analogue on the Thames embankment. The edifice will tower two hundred feet above the desert floor and will be equipped with accommodations for hundreds of Concession agents, its workmanship expressing the century's highest ideals of structural beauty. A simple colonnade of the Tuscan order will sweep beneath its wings; Ionic columns and pediments will cap the building's upper stories. Ballard may summon whatever muscle and material is necessary to have it constructed before June 1895, so that it may be properly furnished for the interplanetary travelers' arrival. Tons of Portland stone have already been cut and shipped.

Burdened by overcoats, impatient with celebratory dinners, and fatigued with London, Ballard is pleased to accept the new assignment. He makes the arrangements to return tens of thousands of fellahin to Point A and set them to work, protected now by a British battalion. A chartered express conveys him to Marseilles, where he boards a military packet to Egypt. At

Alexandria he joins the supplies caravan south through the
"Valley of Rushes," El-Maghra, past the rocky plateau of B'ir
Abu Gharadiq and the Sitra Oasis, and across the greater portion of the Bahr ar Rimal al 'Azim, the Great Sand Sea, and he
recognizes how much he has missed the desert in the last several months: its soundlessness, its blankness. He misses Thayer
no less.

But he's stunned by the sight of the astronomer, who stands
outside his tent as the caravan arrives, in the full sun, as haggard
as a penny-ante fakir, with a fakir's wide-eyed stare. Thayer
doesn't immediately recognize him. The Arab girl doesn't seem
to have fared any better, besides being freakishly hairless. She's
also visibly with child: the most striking measure of Thayer's
decline. Yet the greatest shock is Miss Keaton. She's lost weight
as well as stature; he perceives tremors and confusion. One of
the engineer's first commands provides them with an arriving
Sister of Mercy.

Soon Point A is again the center of an infernal tumult. Thousands swing their hammers at once. Thousands more lift their
burdens. The tower rises from a swarm of shouts and cries. Despite the building's reported solidity—the thousands of tons of
marble that are carted there, the entire forests of mahogany—it
retains a kind of immateriality in the desert astringence. Perhaps
the overwhelming volume of the sky and its purpling deepness
are what make us believe we can see directly behind the structure. Oriented south to face the tracks of the sun, the moon, Mars,
and the other planets, the customs house occupies a magnifi-
cent cobblestoned plaza half a mile wide that would have been
admired in Vienna or Budapest; indeed, many of the cobble-

stones were quarried from Vienna's and Budapest's city squares. Beyond the edge of the pavement lies the duned wastes.

Returning engineers and other Europeans marvel at the transformation that has been wrought so thoroughly that they can't locate their former quarters, nor the old hammam, nor the scaffold. New buildings of brick and mortar are being raised into permanence around the customs house, which nevertheless retains its colorless translucence, and from a distance appears slightly removed from the desert floor, almost hovering there. Only the sun and the sky have remained where they were. The fellahin may not even be aware that they've come back to Point A.

From his movable chair, Thayer witnesses this construction with satisfaction, the men straining against the pull of terrestrial gravity, the days and nights of preparations. The girl brings him to the telescope one evening, an occasion for him to declare that the northern ice cap has greatly diminished and at the junction of nine canals the oasis of Trivium Charontis, or the "Crossroads of Charon," is in full bloom. Ice water gurgles through channels natural and artificial. Tender shoots pierce the red soil. Avians fledge. Spring has come to Mars' northern hemisphere.

△

Accompanied by orchestral fanfare and the Board of Governors, an invigorated Sir Harry arrives to take charge of the Concession's bureau. He must also arrange for the comfort of the heads of state and the returning Khedive, who will meet the Martian representatives. When he surveys the tasks at hand, he

KEN KALFUS

does so with measures of resolve and jubilation. Every thought of the astronomer, however, passes over him like the moon's shadow.

Miss Keaton is yet another shade. She finds him one afternoon in the vast long hall of the unfinished customs house. Torrents of light and heat pour through the leaded clerestory windows. Ballard has so far been unable to solve the problem of keeping the building tolerably cool. The summer solstice is weeks away. She says to Sir Harry, "I presume you're aware that Professor Thayer's name has been excluded from the welcoming commission."

He has anticipated this moment, even if he did not expect the lady to be so frail, her voice so hoarse, and her eyes so fierce. He's taken aback.

"Professor Thayer has been indisposed . . ."

"He's recovering," she declares, even though the astronomer has not left his quarters in the past week, since making his most recent observations.

"His health is our paramount concern."

"I can't conceive how you plan to develop relations with Mars without the man who initiated them!"

Sir Harry smiles, demonstrating his wellborn charm despite the perspiration that has flushed his face and soaked his shirt and jacket.

"Can I offer you some tea, or a cold drink, my dear? There's no ice, I'm afraid. Of course, Professor Thayer is a world hero. The Equilateral was his idea, and without his effort and sacrifices—and certainly your steadfastness, Miss Keaton—not a spadeful of sand would have been turned."

"This is all the more reason for Professor Thayer to be present at the arrival of the Martian delegates. The press will demand it. So will the public. So will Mars!"

"But Professor Thayer is a scientist," Sir Harry says firmly. His eyes bear down on the woman. "And the Equilateral is no longer a scientific concern. The interests of the Concession are strictly commercial. We have obligations to our shareholders, as well as a solemn agreement with the Khedive. In return for the vast improvements the excavation of the Equilateral has brought to his nation, as well as a percentage of future revenue, the Concession has been granted a monopoly on trade with Mars. The Concession will hold the terrestrial patent for Martian inventions. Now that our enterprise has fully assumed its mercantile aspect, men of business will have to take center stage. I'll be the one to meet the embassy, with Herr Krupp, Mr. Rockefeller, and Baron Rothschild at my side. Professor Thayer will be welcome, once he feels fit, to engage his Martian colleagues in discussion of scientific matters, as long as they're without application."

"This can't be!" she protests, realizing at once that it can. She searches his face for a sign that he will soften his heart. "The Equilateral is meant to serve humanity—"

"Millions have been raised for the endeavor, Miss Keaton. The investors expect to profit."

She shudders in response. A tremor pulses through Sir Harry as well: sympathy. He never should have allowed Thayer to keep her in the desert. But the governors were unanimous in their decision to bar Thayer from the commission.

Miss Keaton leaves the customs house without ceremony, a

tiny figure beneath the vastness of Point A's constructions, within the barren enormousness of the Western Desert, under the immense dish of the ceramic sky. She recognizes now that the purposes of the Concession have been visible all the time.

She doesn't inform Thayer about the composition of the welcoming commission. He sleeps most of the day anyway, dreaming of a basic language that he may share with his visitors. He murmurs of diameters and ellipses, of octagons and parabolas, of trapezoids and dodecahedrons.

THIRTY-TWO

I n this glorious culmination of nineteenth-century engineering, organization, and muscle, the customs house is completed—two frenzied weeks into the month of June, but before any sign of the vessels that will arrive from Mars. The Khedive comes with an entourage three times as large as the one that brought him previously. His line of camels sways to the horizon. The viceroy is shortly followed by European prime ministers and heads of state, along with men of industry and ambassadors assigned to relations with Mars. Accommodations consistent with their positions and honors have been constructed for them all. Point A, this formerly anonymous point in the desert, now witnesses the greatest convocation of temporal power since the Congress of Vienna. The newspapers speculate that to ensure political order within the solar system an interplanetary Metternich will have to emerge from the rising city at the Vertex.

The political delegations are shadowed by the many leading astronomers who establish temporary observatories along Point A's unlit outer perimeter, where they hotly contest each other for the first glints of sunlight dimly reflected off the surfaces of the Martian vessels. Thayer has calculated that the fleet's trajectory will pass to the edge of Pisces, perform a slight retrograde pirouette, and then glide through Gemini, Cancer, and Leo for the descent to Earth. The astronomers fix their stare on the loving twins, the scuttling crab, and the imperial lion. The year 1895 will reveal a wealth of asteroids, planetary satellites, double stars, clusters, and nebulae. But every tentative sighting of the travelers from Mars, announced in the night, communicated across Point A's outskirts by high-stepping runners, welcomed, doubted, and disputed by men who strain against the limits of sight at their own eyepieces, remains unconfirmed.

Miss Keaton tells Thayer of the celestial discoveries. Sometimes the astronomer simply nods, as if he isn't listening, but on certain days when the fever has subsided and his eyes clear, he demands their details. When the secretary tells him that Professor Hockstader has reported a seventh-magnitude comet in Virgo, Thayer snorts.

"Has he announced its orbital elements?"

Miss Keaton looks at her notes. The comet hunter's deductions are based on its passage through the constellation over the past three nights. "Mean daily motion, eleven minutes. Perihelion, one-point-five astronomical units. Orbital period, two-point-eight years."

"Doubtful," Thayer says, working up a grin. "It can't be moving that fast. Hockstader's a good observer, but no mathematician. I wouldn't trust him to make change from a pound note."

"The numbers haven't been verified."

"They won't be," he declares.

Thayer is quiet for a few minutes, his forehead creased. He isn't falling asleep.

He says at last, "I bet they're getting impatient."

"Who?"

"About the Martian vessels. They haven't seen them yet, have they? They're looking in Leo's every nook and cranny. No ships?"

Miss Keaton doesn't respond. She has refrained from reporting the astronomers' increasing uneasiness, which is joined by an even greater restlessness among the statesmen and Concession governors who have come to Point A. The European newspapers are publishing leaders with headings like WHERE ARE THEY?

"They *can't* see them!"

"Professor Verzola has been assembling his eleven-inch refractor. He says he'll be ready to observe this evening."

"I've performed new calculations. In my head."

His cheeks and temples are flushed now and he's speaking in a hoarse shout. His stare is not directly at her.

"You have to rest, Pho. There's no need to calculate in your head," she says. She adds, after taking a moment to clear something stuck in her throat, "I'm here, you know."

"The ships from Mars won't be any brighter than the twelfth magnitude until they're almost upon us. None of these instruments, not even Verzola's, will pick them up, certainly not with his vision. The man needs glasses. Twelfth magnitude, Dee!"

"All right, I'll tell them."

"And they won't show up on any plates either. They shouldn't waste their film."

△

As the days pass in unremitting sun, the statesmen of Europe meet to exchange views on terrestrial concerns, especially unrest in the Transvaal and loans to China. Certain levers of power are softly pressed. Borders in the Balkans are quietly redrawn. Populations are shifted. Sums are debited and credited to the accounts of distant banks. A royal engagement is arranged; so is an assassination.

Although Ballard's work at Point A is largely done, the momentum of the rush toward completion still runs through him. He finds calm only when he's with Thayer in the astronomer's darkened room, sitting by his bed, smoking, usually when Miss Keaton is elsewhere engaged. Their conversation is desultory, broken by lengthy, dream-soaked pauses, and the two men occasionally revisit the delays in the excavations, for Thayer doesn't recall, from time to time, that the Equilateral was finished last year.

Thayer doesn't inquire about the Arab girl in the next room. She has entered her confinement in some discomfort or pain that the sisters fail to identify or alleviate. They're not a little put out when Miss Keaton, alarmed by her fever, sends for a Bedouin midwife.

The astronomer ceases to speak of the Equilateral, or of his colleagues camped around Point A, or of the planet Mars. Whether or not Ballard or Miss Keaton are with him, his murmurings now roam into space's deepest reaches, often in the direction of the objects he observed from Chile on the 1890 expedition. "It's a pinwheel of gas, three distinct wings, so luminous you may turn them with a sigh. Messier 83, at the edge of the Centaur. A fresh pencil, please . . . The Magellanic Clouds, great nurseries of stars cottoned in a primeval gaseous haze. This is proof, proof positive of the hypothesis that the nebulae coalesce . . ."

On his rounds Ballard ensures that everything he has constructed at Point A—the gasworks, the waterworks, the sewage system—is operating correctly. He inspects the wide processional boulevard, which begins, its stones washed twice a day, at the customs house and terminates at the palace for the visiting heads of state. The palace is modeled on Balmoral. Drawing from the designs of recent constructions like the Reichstag and the Hôtel de Ville, lesser diplomatic and commercial buildings line the road. Ballard searches between and beyond them, into the alkali desolation, for one more thing to build. He avoids the Concession offices, where men from London have come. They're in their offices, writing and reading reports, but they have little to do until the Martian embassy arrives. Among the diplomats he senses a rising tension. They look into his face with questions; when they step outside, they can't help but lift their heads to the vacant sky.

Three weeks after the day in which the ships were expected to land, the mood shifts decisively. Ballard senses that the impatience rippling beneath the sands of the encampment has curdled into anger. Sir Harry goes quiet, as if his face has been slapped. Perhaps it has been, by one of the other governors or an investor or a member of Parliament. The dignitaries talk of departing Point A, for they have nations and empires to run. There's only so much time that the prime minister of Britain can spend with the president of France before troubles arise somewhere in Africa. The leaders will allow their envoys, or their junior envoys, to attend the travelers, if they come at all. Yet none hurries to leave, fearful of yielding a diplomatic advantage.

The Khedive and his Egyptian retinue have installed themselves in a wing of the palace, in disregard of common diplomatic protocol. On the one hand the Khedive appears to imagine that social intercourse with Egypt will be Mars' primary objective; at the same time he urges his fellow dignitaries to remain at Point A to demonstrate mankind's solidarity. "The visitors from Mars will care little to distinguish either between the Frenchman and the German or the Egyptian and the Englishman," he says, raising hackles up and down the palace's plushly carpeted, electrically lit corridors.

Ballard observes that neither the political leaders nor the Concession's governors require further construction. They're beginning to look for men to blame, and with Thayer absent, the engineer is the most conspicuous of them.

△

Every day the Red Planet sets earlier and a few degrees closer to the sun, which has blazed the path ahead of it into Leo. As seen from Mars, the Earth appears to sink every morning farther into the dawn. On the evening of August 16, 1895, shortly after the onset of dusk, Professor Verzola makes out the last of Mars. He says that by the following evening it will not be

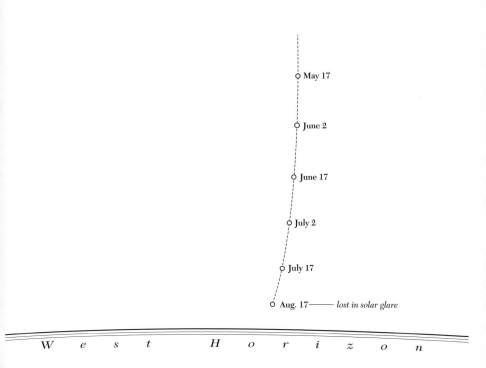

○ May 17

○ June 2

○ June 17

○ July 2

○ July 17

○ Aug. 17——— *lost in solar glare*

W   e   s   t   H   o   r   i   z   o   n

**Mars as seen from Earth, 1895,
end of evening twilight.**

KEN KALFUS

viewable at all. This declaration of heliacal descension, long
foreseen in ephemeridic columns and tables, rumbles through
the city. At daybreak, as blown sand starts to obscure the Equilateral, the British prime minister and the French president
depart for Alexandria in separate caravans. Ballard understands that Sir Harry is in a rage.

That afternoon, with Mars conclusively hidden by the solar
glare, Ballard climbs to the third floor of the infirmary. He recognizes that something is wrong before he reaches the landing.
A low, grinding, worried murmur spills down the stairs. When
he arrives he's confronted by two French nurses outside the
open door to the girl's room, scowling.

The engineer represses his natural squeamishness and looks
in. The small whitewashed room has been occupied by a con-
tingent of robed Bedouin women, their faces hidden. They sur-
round the hospital bed. Ballard can't see the girl. One of the
women must be the midwife. He presumes the others are from
her family and clan. He detects the scent of raw garlic; also of
fenugreek and cardamom.

He goes to Thayer's room.

"Sanford!" he says heartily. "How are you feeling, old man?
We've got a bit of a wind up today."

He drops himself into a chair next to Miss Keaton, before
realizing that he's intruded. They ignore him, or they haven't
noticed his entrance. But the attending sister flares to Ballard
an expression of grave significance.

Thayer's no longer speaking with Miss Keaton about nebulae. Sweat illumines his face and his eyes are as vivacious as a

schoolboy's. He's telling her, "It was a full day's journey from San Pedro, Dee."

"That's right," she says. "About nine hours."

"You rode the frisky bay. The boys made camp on an elevated ridge protected by a stand of mesquite trees. They prepared dinner over the campfire, a chupe stew, fresh beefsteak and rice and red beans, served with a peppery sauce and a cactus salad. Dusk came. We set up the refractor, established polar alignment. There was good-to-excellent seeing. I ranked it a nine on the Douglass Scale. We made our observations, the southern nebulae, the Messiers. When we returned to the fire for warmth, the boys had faded into the distant shadows. We couldn't hear them, save for the occasional melancholy airs of a mouth organ. We were left to ourselves. We couldn't see the stars, the campfire was too intense. We saw only each other. Whatever lies beyond the fire is . . ." Thayer falls silent for several moments. Then he completes the thought: "Unknown."

Ballard doesn't move, not even to exhale. He can't withdraw from the sickroom for fear of drawing attention to himself.

"There's only us," Miss Keaton affirms, whispering.

"Only us," Thayer repeats, closing his eyes for a moment. But still he speaks. "Only the two of us, two minds . . . We've understood each other from the start. We need each other. It's irrefutable."

He opens his eyes. Ballard realizes, with a start, that Thayer can't see at all, yet his eyes remain fixed on Miss Keaton.

Thayer shudders. He's silent for a few minutes before he continues: "Flame light kisses your face, which is completely, boldly open to my gaze. I ask a question, without words, but a gesture, comprising a quarter smile and my direct look, becomes comprehensible by the miracle of concordant intellects. You smile as I've never seen you smile before. I understand your sign in return, which speaks of agreement, and also of trust and kindness. It speaks too of appetite. All that in a smile! We retire to my tent without a word. Our embrace is gentle, but hardly tentative. We fumble with fasteners, but nothing proves awkward, ever."

"Yes, Pho," she says. "That's true."

"And what a discovery, what a revelation. Your sweet, welcoming mouth. The strength of your arms. Your heat. Then, my darling, your graces are offered to my sight and touch. Powerful thighs and delicately turned ankles, the saucy, aggressive rump, hah, I was taken by surprise. The full breasts tipped with dusky aureolas. Your caresses are light and knowing. Your broad freckled back. The mons veneris, moist and warm and hungry and yielding, a perfect fit, dear. Your skin tastes of mesquite, and sweat, and citronella. Yes, my darling, it does."

"Yes," she murmurs.

A foreign howl, a prolonged wail, slices through the sickroom. It reverberates against the walls and shivers the windows. Ballard looks up abruptly, gazing through the open door into the hallway.

Thayer falls silent. The cry, the first time this voice has been heard in this world, has penetrated down, down, down to him. The Chilean desert vanishes. His eyes narrow.

"They've arrived," he whispers, barely audible, and barely in the room. "They're here."

Miss Keaton drops her head and stares into her lap.

Ballard continues to look away, into the hallway. In the corridor the nurses hold their breaths. Carts brake on the plaza before the customs hall. The fellahin put down their packs and look up. A caravan driver raises a bony hand and a long, outstretched finger to order a halt. He listens. Men in offices lift their pencils from their documents and allow them to stay in place, hovering. Diplomats pause in their negotiations. No one speaks as they wait for the next signal, the inevitable call of life; intelligent, companionable, needful, rampant life.

A Note on the Author

△

Ken Kalfus is the author of two novels, *The Commissariat of Enlightenment* and *A Disorder Peculiar to the Country*, which was a finalist for the 2006 National Book Award. He's also published two collections of stories, *Thirst* and *Pu-239 and Other Russian Fantasies*, a finalist for the PEN/Faulkner Award. His books have been translated into more than ten foreign languages. He lives in Philadelphia.

3+ 9/13